The Cat in the Headlights

by

Jon Nikrich

The aforementioned efforts to kill me

I remember the first time that somebody aimed a gun at my head and told me I was about to die. Something about the seriousness of the situation, unprecedented at the time, compelled me to commit its details to memory. To be honest, the 12 times it's happened since are starting to blur into each other.

I have a gift. By gift, I mean a unique personality trait. By unique personality trait, I mean the ability to prompt hatred and occasional homicidal tendencies in an implausibly high percentage of the public. If given a choice, it isn't the gift I would select.

I wasn't born with this skill. It evolved over time. Some of it is due to misunderstandings and some of it to bad luck. Much of it is due to historical events about which I can do nothing. All of it conspires to influence my life in unexpected and frequently near-fatal ways.

I should tell you more about myself so that you have a picture and some context as I describe the attempts on my life.

The first thing you should know about me is that I am a nice guy, or at least I try to be. I hold open doors. I help friends move house. I buy rounds when it's my turn. I'm the type of person who would help an old lady cross the street, by which I mean that I would if anyone still does that.

Have you ever seen anybody help an old lady cross the street? I admit I never have. I think the expression pre-dates zebra crossings and my willing assistance might be superfluous to a traffic light and stripy road markings. However, if I saw an old lady attempting to cross a road unsuccessfully and I thought my involvement might secure her safely to her destination, I would help her.

I would say I am predisposed to being helpful. That's who I am, but that's not the cause of my problems.

Physically, I'm average in height and above average in athleticism due to a dedicated exercise regime that revolves around thwarting efforts to kill me. My intelligence and general knowledge are good and my mental awareness is world class due to the aforementioned efforts to kill me. Psychologically, I'm feeling a little jaded for reasons you can predict if you've followed the pattern of the sentences in this paragraph.

I am reasonably good-looking. I've heard this from enough people that I think it is fair to repeat it. I don't mean that I could be a model, but if you picture your circle of friends, I could be the best-looking guy in that circle. If you and all your friends are 55, picture your children's friends. If you're 80, picture your grandchildren.

In summary, I am handsome enough that many people would instinctively like me, but not so handsome that others would jealously hate me. My looks are also not the cause of my problems. Actually, that last statement isn't completely true. I'll explain that later.

My mouth is sometimes faster than my brain. Now that I think about it, this may be the cause of some of my problems.

Career-wise, I don't really have a career. I am currently between opportunities. If you've heard people use this expression, you'll know it's often a euphemism for recently fired. That's how I use it too. I am fired a lot.

I've worked for a lot of companies in the past two years, including a role I tolerated that paid very little and a role I loved that paid almost nothing. I'm no longer in either. I am rarely idle and I consistently earn a wage, but I change jobs too often to consider any of them as the first stage of a long-term career.

The way it works is as follows:

1. I secure employment with a company.

2. I work hard and impress my colleagues enough that my prior work history confuses them.

3. I earn sufficient goodwill that they like me, but not enough to ignore Ned Dwyer when he tells them that my continued presence would attract his unwelcome influence.

Typically, this third and final step approximates to the four-month anniversary of my recruitment. The timing depends on how much attention Ned is paying.

Ned Dwyer is a big deal in my town. There isn't much he can't arrange if he sets his mind to it. This is unfortunate because what he sometimes sets his mind to is selecting a piece of my life and arranging its deterioration. The discontinuation of my employment is his favourite expression of involvement.

I'm not sure what to tell you about my love life. I spent most of the past year between relationships. If you've heard people use this expression, you'll know it's often a euphemism for a recent break-up. That's how I use it too. I'm on the wrong side of a lot of break-ups.

In terms of family, I have a mother, a half-brother and a half-sister. My family is dysfunctional. By most criteria, we're not a family.

I love my brother more than almost anything, although he is what I would affectionately term a screw-up. He would laugh at that designation and argue the case for something stronger on the basis that it unfairly fails to consider some of his mistakes. He has a long history of mistakes.

I love many things more than my sister and she is what I would critically term a screw-up. She would take offense at that designation and argue the case for something milder on the basis that the description hurts her feelings. She has a long history of hurt feelings.

My mother is too complicated to summarize in an introduction. For now, assume you won't like her.

Finally, I should mention that most people call me Ray. It's actually my surname, but it's what I quote to the people I meet. I have another name to go before this and I quote it to as few people as possible.

I like to think that if you met me, you'd like me. I can't guarantee it.

I know that at this stage I've only given you a snapshot to work with. You may wonder how it is that someone like me could provoke 13 attempts on his life. That's the first misconception I should clarify. 13 is the number of times someone has aimed a gun at my head and told me I was about to die. The number is higher if you include the gun-related threats against other vital organs. I couldn't even guess the total if you included the occasions someone waved a gun at me and didn't clearly articulate his or her intent.

I can't share every tale I've lived to tell. However, if you'll permit me, I will share the story of last year. I think it's the obvious choice because there have been somewhere in the region of 157 attempts on my life and last year features 62 of them.

My established strategy of hating you

I read somewhere that you should never open a story with the central character losing his job or his girlfriend as a justification for the events that follow. I understand the principle, but I lose both so frequently, it's difficult for me to choose a starting point that doesn't involve one or the other.

It was the first Tuesday of the year. It was my first day of work after the break because New Year's Day had fallen on a Saturday and donated the public holiday to the Monday. I got up later than I intended and I was running late. As I tried to leave, some suitcases blocked my route to the front door.

Only two people lived in the house and there were too many cases for an impromptu holiday. I jumped to some conclusions. My guesses were disappointingly accurate.

Caitlyn Asher, my home's only other resident, watched me watch the cases. She'd thought through all kinds of ways she could broach the subject, struggled to find her thousand words and gone with a picture instead.

I'd like to give due credit to her luggage. They conveyed her news very effectively.

I was surprised and I had every right to be. I was not a bad boyfriend, myopic to the unhappiness of a long-suffering girlfriend. I knew she was unhappy, but I also knew I wasn't the cause of her unhappiness. I'd expected some changes. I hadn't expected to be one of them.

Before I go on, I should tell you more about Caitlyn because she's in the story again.

She's beautiful. I've heard this from enough people that I think it's fair to repeat it. I don't mean that she could be a model, but she could be that girl from your school who was clearly more attractive than the rest of her graduate class and still is a decade and a half later. In Caitlyn's school, it was Caitlyn. In summary, she is beautiful enough that many people instinctively hate her.

At her best, she's too good for me. It's not even close. Ironically, it's when she's at her best that she wants to be with me. It's when she's stressed and overwhelmed that she leaves me.

Prior to our suitcase-inspired conversation, we'd been together for four years, on and off. She'd walked out before. Suitcases were a new development. They suggested planning. They suggested a more serious split than the ones we'd worked through previously.

I don't recall everything we said that morning. I think the general themes were her intention to leave and my intention to remain confused by her departure. We ultimately achieved both. I remember how it ended.

"I think you're making a mistake." I said, not for the first time.

"It's complicated. I tried to explain."

"I know, but I don't understand. You love me?"

"Yes."

"But you're unhappy with your stressful job, tyrannical boss, difficult family, unreliable friends, personal finances and self-image."

"... Yes."

"And you're dropping the good part of your life to devote more time to the bad."

She nodded weakly.

"Oh ... Then I did understand."

If I had known in advance that these would be my last words before she closed the door, I would have chosen something other than 'I did understand'.

It wasn't even true. I was still confused.

Two hours later, I walked into my editor's office. I worked part time for a local paper, a job I loved.

I thought I was there to discuss my late arrival and I had my excuses ready. Aaron Hayes, the senior editor, liked Caitlyn. I knew any explanation that involved our separation would distract him from further discussion of my lateness.

Before I go on, I should tell you more about Aaron because he's in the story again.

The first thing I should tell you is that he's not fat. He's tubby. He's moderately overweight. I wouldn't mention his size as a characteristic except that he's so aware that he's moderately overweight that it influences his whole personality.

It affects his self-confidence. His lack of self-confidence affects his professional success. His lack of professional success prompts his father to help him repeatedly. His reliance on his father cripples his self-esteem and undermines his self-confidence.

He's also a terrible driver. This is independent of all of the above. He's crashed eight times in the past four years and there may be more I don't know about. If the company cars of our country formed a union, their first demand would be a refusal to work with Aaron.

Aaron's father owns the paper. In an effort to promote readership outside of the area, he set it up to emphasize online content and humour. I wrote a facetious, satirical column for their website and in return received a company car, a company phone and no wages whatsoever.

Incidentally, this is the only job that Ned never interfered with. I think he knew they didn't actually pay me.

Aaron's father owns a car rental business, a mobile phone store and several other diverse businesses. In the place of financial reward, he compensated most of the newspaper's staff in merchandise from other parts of his faltering empire. I can't say with any certainty that he paid anybody other than his son.

There was a period, a very long time ago, that Aaron and I were friends. He denies this now, but it's true. He made an effort because the paper needed me and his dad told him to. I made an effort because I officially worked for him, I unofficially worked for his dad and I enjoyed the job. It wasn't much effort. It was a real friendship. Then he met Caitlyn.

They met at a party. He said something like "I don't know you and I don't know anything about you, but I know we're meant to be together."

It wasn't a line. He genuinely believed it. He genuinely believed it for a very long time. Caitlyn didn't. She politely advised him of this several times over several years.

Her feelings for him could best be described as a hybrid of embarrassment and indifference. At the same time, she wouldn't hear a word of criticism against him. I think it alleviated her guilt for how much he adored her and how she didn't in return.

I first heard about his infatuation several weeks after his first profession of affection. It was on my fourth date with Caitlyn. I'd met her at the same party and asked her out at the end of the evening. I was completely unaware of his feelings for her until she told me the story. This piece of information went someway to explaining his sudden resentment of me, the origin of which I'd been trying to determine for several weeks.

This resentment manifested itself in a couple of ways. The principal among these was that he'd started discussing me with my colleagues, usually with leading statements such as the company's overreliance on my overrated writing.

That morning, in the context of how he liked Caitlyn and disliked me, I thought he would accept my prepared excuses. I didn't get a chance to offer them because he started the conversation by firing me.

"What? Why?"

"It's mostly because I hate you." he replied. "I've always hated you. No, that's not true. I haven't always hated you, but I've hated you for long enough that I'm comfortable using always as a suitable replacement for whatever period of time it is that I've hated you. I've finally found an outlet for my hatred."

"I'm your most popular writer."

"Mal McCall is my most popular writer."

"I write that column. Mal McCall doesn't exist."

"He exists to his readers and that's all that matters. A national tabloid approached me several weeks ago and they want to hire him as a feature writer for a new column."

"Did you tell them he's fictional?"

"They already knew. They want to buy into Mal's following. They are purchasing Mal's name and they have a team of writers who'll produce the column. The deal is we don't replace the column with anything similar. As such, I no longer need you, which requires that I fire you, which fits in with my established strategy of hating you. Besides, I wrote off another car and I want yours."

"You can't do this."

"No, I'm thinking I can. I'll need your company mobile and your car keys."

It is fair to say that since this conversation, I have wished him misfortune.

Before she left me, Caitlyn told me on several occasions that I was too hard on Aaron. My dismissal was my opportunity to disregard her persistent defence of his character for the following reasons.

1. She was indirectly responsible for the degree to which he despised me.

2. She would find it exponentially more difficult to defend Aaron if her immediate plans involved her absence from all of our conversations.

3. If someone fires you, you automatically acquire permission to wish that person whatever misfortune you deem appropriate. I'm fairly sure that's a rule.

Two hours later, I was sitting on the bottom step of the staircase in my hallway, my head in my lap, a phone in my hand, the unappreciative recipient of a dinner invitation from my mother.

If you'd asked me four days prior to this for my resolutions, I would have replied that all I wanted from life was three things. The polar opposite of those three things are a break-up, unemployment and a meal at my mother's house.

"It's not a good idea."

"It's only a dinner. What's wrong with us acting like family?"

"It's wrong because we act like a family who hate each other. Most days you curse the fact I exist. On the isolated days you feel bad about that you want reconciliation. The problem is that by the laws of probability, there's an excellent chance you'll be cursing me again on the day I visit."

"Please come for dinner. I promise I'll try this time."

"What about Rob?"

"Yes, I've invited your sister and her boyfriend." my mum replied.

My sister, Roberta, and my mother adore each other. They have an unbreakable mother-daughter bond that withstands every storm life throws at them. It is fair to say that my mother considers me a storm life threw at them. I can't provide further details as I've yet to determine a reason for anyone to adore my sister.

"Is she still with the psychotic?" I asked.

"Gary? No. That ended a week ago. She's with a completely different psychotic now."

"Did you know Gary wants me dead?"

"No. What did you do?"

"I warned Rob that he might become violent. Gary took offence and threatened to kill me. Do you know of anyone with worse taste in men?"

"Be nice. She's your sister."

"When you have a day like mine, you get a pass. I don't have to be nice to anybody."

The crazy people my hometown boasts

Before I go on, I should tell you about Gary Grey because he's in this story a lot.

There are people you can recognize from a distance before you see their faces. Gary's like that. He's unique in the way he carries himself, the way he walks, the way he does everything. I've tried to explain this uniqueness to people before and the best I can offer is that Gary isn't right.

When I say he isn't right, I don't mean that he's always wrong. Yes, he's frequently wrong. I would even say he's wrong a statistically improbable percentage of the time, but Gary flukes on the truth occasionally. No, I mean he isn't right. There's a synapse misfiring or a key cell missing. You know it the first time you meet him. You can't define it easily, you can't describe it perfectly, but you meet him and you sense it.

He has a way of viewing the world. He doesn't realize that his view is unique. He doesn't realize that his view is completely inaccurate.

He's physically interesting too. He's disconcertingly skinny. It's not an athletic leanness. It's a dietary regime that revolves around forgetting to eat. I heard that he has issues with metabolism. I can't remember who told me that, but I tend to believe any sentence that includes the words Gary and issues.

It's possible that if scientists studying evolution got a good look at him, it would blow away their theories and set them back a couple of centuries. I think they'd probably hush up his existence to avoid the scandal of how his existence discredits their work.

Before she left him, Rob told me on several occasions that I was too hard on Gary. I dismissed her momentary defence of his character for the following reasons.

1. She places a subconscious and unofficial time limit on all her boyfriends. It's easier to await the inevitable than change her mind.

2. She is a terrible judge of character.

3. She is terrible judge of everything else.

I saw Gary the same day I was fired, dumped and offered some homemade cooking. I visited a local pub called the Village Idiot, named ironically for the successful school dropout who owned it. Like most of the locals, I shortened it to The Idiot. I hadn't been there in years because Caitlyn didn't like its name and refused to drink there. I picked it that day because I needed to think through recent events before I spoke to her again and it was somewhere I was certain I wouldn't see her.

I sat on a stool at the bar. The only customers were in the booths near the right wall. The barman struggled to find enough work to keep busy and sparked some conversation.

"Drinking alone?" he asked.

"I called up some people. They said they want to stay friends with my ex-girlfriend and me. Drinking with me could be seen as choosing sides and they don't want to do that.

"OK. You know what they're saying though?"

"They're choosing sides and they've chosen hers."

"Good. At least you know."

I asked for a pity pint and the barman pulled me a glass of the on-tap beer.

"It's not a pity pint. Your column makes me laugh. You're Mal McCall, right?"

"I used to be."

"You're changing your name?

"No, my real name isn't Mal."

"But you write as Mal."

"Yes. But it isn't my name."

"Then why do you write as Mal?"

"It sounds better than my name."

"So why are you changing it?"

"I don't own it."

"You don't own your name?"

"No, the paper sold it."

"They sold your name? Who to?"

"Another paper."

"But they didn't buy you?"

"They didn't want me. They just wanted my name."

"How come you don't own the name?"

"I never owned it."

"But you own your real name?"

"Yes, but I never use it."

"Why?"

"I don't like it."

"You have a name you own and don't like and a name you like and don't own and you need a new name so you don't have to use the name you don't own or the name you got when you were named?"

"Yes."

"That makes my head hurt. When you drink here, your name's Mal."

The barman looked up as a potential customer walked in. I saw Gary Grey in the mirror that hung on the back wall. He approached the barman and I glanced at him without drawing attention.

Gary looked skinnier than usual. He looked scruffier too. It was either a token effort at disguising his appearance or he'd forgotten to wash when he was busy forgetting to eat.

"I'm looking for a guy by the name of Ray." Gary said. "I heard he was here."

I didn't understand at the time why he didn't recognize me. We'd met on at least five occasions. There were several possible explanations and I incorrectly credited it to stupidity. This was a mistake on my part, but it's one you'd understand if you've ever met Gary.

"Ray? I don't think I know anyone called Ray." the barman said.

He turned to me, a slight smile on his face that Gary missed.

"Hey, Mal. You know anyone called Ray?"

I shook my head and kept my gaze on the bar. I'm not scared of Gary, but I also had no interest in talking with him. He took another quick look at me and then left. The barman waited until after Gary's departure and then confirmed what he already suspected.

"Mal, whose name isn't Mal, is your name Ray?"

"Sometimes."

"You better go the back way. There's something about that guy, something not right."

The chef at The Idiot is insane. He is emotionally attached to machetes, aprons and all the other elements that are synonymous with his profession. He wanders to and from work in his kitchen garb, sometimes covered in the remnants of whatever he chopped that day, machete still in hand. It's alarming the first time you encounter him this way, but I dismiss his eccentricity as harmless. It's a courteous designation I extend to every crazy person my hometown boasts who's never tried to hurt me.

As I entered the kitchen, he picked up a bag of rubbish, violently kicked the back door open and threw the bag into a skip on the far side of the alley. He turned to scald whoever had invaded his sovereign territory, but he held his tongue when he recognized me. We know each other a little because, like most of the crazy people my hometown boasts, he briefly dated my sister.

"The barman said I could leave this way. I'm trying to avoid someone."

"You wouldn't be the first." he acknowledged. "How are you Ray?"

"I've been better."

"Me too. I'm in a battle of wills with a local stray and he's winning. Do me a favour. Shout me if you see a scruffy-looking mongrel nosing through our rubbish."

I agreed. It seemed a fair trade for an escape route.

The chef took another bag, kicked the door so that it shook on its hinges and hurled the bag accurately into the centre of the skip. It was a perfect throw. The door closed slowly and he returned to other tasks.

I paused until I was sure my exit wouldn't coincide with more tidying. The way my day had progressed, I could clearly picture a bag of garbage knocking me unconscious as I passed the skip.

I left through the door and turned towards the lights of the main road.

"I knew it was you." Gary said.

I looked back down the alley as he stepped out of the shadows. He leaned into the wall near to the kitchen door.

"Gary. Small world. How are things?"

"Things? Things aren't good. I can't sleep. I'm not eating. All I can think about is the last ten weeks. I'd finally met someone special and I was happy."

"Sorry, can I check? When you say someone special, do you mean my sister?"

"Is that a joke? Your sister is wonderful."

"I don't want to disagree with you, though mostly because you're deluded and violent. I'll give it a shot anyway. Rob's never seen anyone for more than three months. You lasted ten weeks, which isn't bad. You came out of it with a high opinion of her, which may be a first. And she ignores my opinions, so if you think I had any influence on your breakup …"

"I think you had everything to do with it."

He slowly lifted his jacket and pulled a gun from the back of his jeans.

"I told her you were prone to violence. You're not proving me wrong."

"I think you've said enough. If you've got last words, you should say them."

A scrawny dog passed between us and walked towards the alley's newest rubbish bags.

"Dog." I said.

Gary smiled.

"Really? That's your last word?"

"Dog." I shouted.

The kitchen door flew open and hit Gary in the face. The scrawny canine jumped from the skip and dashed into the darkness of the alley. The chef sprinted after him.

The door drifted shut slowly and revealed Gary's unconscious body. I picked up the gun, threw it into the skip and piled some rubbish bags on top of it.

I was calmer than you might expect. As I've already mentioned, it wasn't the first time that somebody had considered shooting me. I treated it as another small piece of a Tuesday that had been, until that point, consistently disappointing. On reflection, the confrontation with Gary wasn't even the worst part of my day.

It started to rain.

More dead than I like to be

I grew up in a town called Markden. In a quirk of disparity between how we say it and how we spell it, we pronounce it as Marden. There is a long and tedious explanation for why the K is silent, but I will spare you the details. I wish Markden's schools had extended generations of students the same offer.

Incidentally, we're not the only English location to include additional, unnecessary letters in our name. Decreeing less than obvious pronunciations for some of its towns is something at which the English truly excel. Unfortunately, Markden's only claim to fame is the ferocity of its weather.

If I tell you that my birthplace specializes in rain, my misleading understatement does it great disservice. Its weather system is split evenly between torrential downpours and ominous clouds that hint at all the hard work and preparation required to produce the torrential downpours to follow.

Fortunately, a lifetime of living here has prepared Markden's occupants for the weather we endure. We're impervious to rain and we never catch colds. It's a neat trick that would make us millions if we could bottle it.

It was because of this that when it started to rain, I knew something heavier was inevitable. In the absence of the car I'd recently surrendered at Aaron's request, I had no choice but to attempt my fifteen-minute trek home in the storm.

I turned up my collar and tucked my arms tightly into my chest. I vaguely noticed the car with tinted windows as it passed in the opposite direction. I missed the illegal U-turn it completed to return in my direction. I finally granted it the attention it deserved as it slowed to a halt alongside me.

The front passenger door opened and a very tall man climbed out. He had a physique that seemed suitable for a career in hurting people and I immediately assumed that he worked for Ned Dwyer. Ned recruits a lot of people with this physique. He employs a lot of people who hurt people.

Ned considers my life to be a pet project and he likes to meddle with it. Sometimes he is creative in how he meddles. Sometimes he doesn't have the time or energy for original ideas and he resorts to a default strategy that involves one of his employees hitting me repeatedly. As I already mentioned, he has staff well suited to this strategy. The passenger from the car was large enough.

"This can't be happening." I said.

This was a basic admission of disappointment and not a fair interpretation of events. It could be happening. It has happened. Over the years, it's happened a lot.

I looked in both directions for an escape route, albeit half-heartedly. I could have run, but they would have caught me eventually. I've learned from experience not to antagonize Ned's people when their general intent is to hurt me. I have no hard data or statistical models to back it up, but it is my belief that there is a direct correlation between how much I provoke them and the seriousness of the beating they eventually administer.

The man towered over me and glared down from an angle that appeared to be uncomfortable for his neck. When he spoke, his voice was deep, much as you would expect from an intimidating and potentially violent man. His serious frown suggested unhappiness, perhaps with the weather, perhaps with the uncomfortable angle of his neck.

"Get in the car."

"I don't expect sympathy."

"Get in the car."

"I know you can make my day worse, but you really don't have to. It's bad enough already. You can save yourself the trouble, safe in the knowledge that this will still be my worst day ever."

"Don't think I'm not listening but …"

"Get in the car?"

"Get in the car."

He opened the back door for me and I hesitated for a few more seconds. I wondered why they needed me in the vehicle. It was unlikely that Ned had graced the assault with his presence. I assumed that they wanted to take me to an isolated location that also provided shelter from the storm. In this way, they could complete their assignment without getting wetter than absolutely necessary.

I took a deep breath and climbed inside. As the door closed behind me, the back seat's other occupant looked at my haggard expression and soaked clothing. He grinned in response.

"Watch out, little brother. Your day just got better."

For a few moments, we hugged and laughed hysterically. I was all the more ecstatic because the unexpected reunion was such a reversal from what I'd expected. By this stage, the car was moving and I honestly can't tell you when it set off.

My brother Warwick looks a bit like me. Actually, I'm younger than he is, so maybe that's unfair. I look a lot like him. We're not identical, but the likeness is close enough that I've had complete strangers ask me if Warwick Ray is a relative.

He's taller than I am. He's heavier. He has the biggest grin in the world and a nose that's been punched in a few directions it was never intended to go. Other than Caitlyn, there's no one I love more in the world. I hadn't seen him since his return to prison, a place he relocates to so regularly that he's on first name terms with every long-term inmate and every member of staff.

I waited until we finished laughing before starting and failing to finish the obvious question.

"I can't tell you how happy I am to see you, but you're …"

"It's a long story. The short version includes a conditional release."

He nodded his head at the tall men in the front seat. My initial excitement faded as I took in the implications of his hint.

"You turned?"

Warwick's smile disappeared. It takes a lot to make his smile disappear. I'm ashamed to say I accomplished it.

"I had Ned's back. He could have counted on me 100% and I thought I'd shown him that. Then, for some reason, he got nervous about how much I knew. He tried to do something about it that would have left me more dead than I like to be. I'm working with the only option he left me and I'm talking about him for a Get Out Of Jail Free card. You're not going to say I did the wrong thing?"

"No. No. But I am wondering what Ned might do when he finds out you're out."

"Yeah. I know."

"You're OK though?"

"I'm fine."

"It's great to see you."

"It's great to be seen." he replied. "How's my little brother's perfect life?"

"It's not so perfect. Caitlyn left me, Aaron fired me, I got invited to a family dinner, my sister's ex attacked me and it rained a lot."

"That's a rough week."

"That's the last six hours. But I got to see you. Maybe you're the start of things going right."

"I might not be. When Ned finds out, it might bring some trouble your way."

"Ned has hated me a long time and I'm still around."

"I hope your week gets better."

"It just did."

I said it. I'm glad I said it because it brought his smile back. I can't promise I meant it.

The stupidest man on the planet

I was excited to see my brother, but I knew that Ned would cause trouble for me if he thought I knew Warwick's location. Possible attention from Ned Dwyer scared me more than certain attention from Gary Grey.

Gary's anger hadn't faded since his unsuccessful attempt on my life. He'd decided that my death was his new life goal and, for some reason, his broken nose and black eye hadn't dissuaded him from this.

I saw him exactly a week after the incident in the alley. He skipped the detailed justification of his actions and the premature monologue of his victory. Instead, he attempted to complete his assault in the minimum amount of time, drew his weapon in clumsy haste and accidentally shot himself in the foot.

I decided against telling the police for the second time that month. Reporting Gary's behaviour is a waste of time. In addition to being Gary's uncles, Desmond, Dominic and Donald Buckler are Markden police officers who routinely cover for him.

Des, Dom and Don disliked me from the second they knew about me, mostly because Gary suggested it. On the plus side, they never tried to kill me, and I mention this because they would probably have been good at it. It's true that Gary tried enough for all of them, but I wasn't worried. If I had someone trying to kill me, it might as well be the stupidest man on the planet.

I carried on as normal. I applied for jobs. I tried to contact Caitlyn.

If this were a movie, there would now be a montage to convey the repetitive and frustrating experience of the many, many phone calls that filled the next week.

I would like to provide an estimate of the number of times I uttered the following expressions.

1. I'm calling about the advertised position. (Estimated instances 41)

2. Thank you for your time. (Estimated instances 41)

3. Caitlyn, please, don't hang up. (Estimated instances 6)

I switched into a new daily routine. I walked to the nearest store. I bought the daily papers and scanned the classifieds for opportunities. I read the papers from the bottom step of my staircase, the nearest makeshift seat to the telephone in my hallway.

In an ideal world, I would have completed my research from the relative comfort of my dining room table with the papers spread out in front of me. Unfortunately, my hall phone was the only one I owned since Aaron's reclamation of my company mobile and car.

I liked staying near the phone for incoming messages. I hoped optimistically for invitations from prospective employers and reconciliation with my ex-girlfriend. Unfortunately, the morning's calls arrived from less welcome sources.

"Hello." I said.

"What did you do to Gary?" my sister shrieked. "He's in hospital. He's in a lot of pain."

My sister survives in an unhealthy state of semi-permanent hysteria. Some of it is an act as a means of getting her way. Some of it is a genuine misinterpretation of circumstances and an overreaction to her false conclusions. I deduced this decades ago. My mother never will.

"Rob, he …"

"I can't believe you'd hurt him like this. You're so …"

I put the phone down and returned to my classifieds. I circled one ad and gave another an ambiguous question mark that I would cross out as unrealistic later that day. I scribbled over the article announcing Mal McCall's resignation and his new opportunity with a national newspaper. The phone rang again.

"Hello."

"You put the phone down on your sister."

"Mum, she …"

"She's very upset. She …"

I hung up again.

I'd resolved that morning to stay by the phone until I received at least one piece of good news. Ironically, it was phone calls that drove me away from the hallway and into Markden's town centre.

The term town centre might conjure the wrong image. Markden's centre is a street and a traffic jam. Our Chinatown is a restaurant. Our entertainment district is a multiplex with two working screens. It's part of our heritage that we talk about our town like it's bigger than it is. It's a communal joke and one that I simultaneously promoted and ridiculed as Mal McCall.

A loud bang, like someone hitting metal with a hammer, interrupted my temporary excursion. I turned to see a driving instructor's car weave left and right in the fashion of a nervous beginner driver. It narrowly swerved out of the path of an oncoming bus before disappearing into the distance. I made a mental note to never become a driving instructor.

Despite the misfortune this represented for someone else, I was relieved to see an explanation with which I wasn't connected. It spoke to my month, and my increasing pessimism, that I interpreted each unexpected noise as somehow connected with me and with some form of danger.

A passing stranger pulled me from my thoughts.

"Hey, Mal, I heard about your new job. Well done."

"Thanks. I'm not really …"

The stranger walked away and ignored my reply. This wasn't the last time that someone congratulated me on Mal's success. Most of the locals who read the column thought I was Mal or else associated me with it so strongly that they believed that I would share in his good news. I heard congratulations on a daily basis for the next month.

A car with tinted windows pulled alongside me and I escaped from my untidy life into the mess that belonged to my brother. I climbed inside and the vehicle pulled back into the traffic jam.

"How are you?" I asked.

"I'm getting sucked into daytime television. Other than that, not bad. You?"

"My sister's ex wants to kill me."

"Do I know him?"

"Gary Grey."

"Kind of skinny? Kind of ugly?"

"That's the one."

"It must be hard looking over your shoulder the whole time."

"It's not as bad as it sounds. He's working set shifts at the moment so I only have to watch out weekends and Tuesday afternoons."

The car took its second right turn in as many minutes and I recognised it as a flying visit. I predicted they would drop me on the piece of pavement where they'd collected me.

"I never liked Gary." Warwick said. "He's completely devoid of qualities. I'm surprised it took your sister 24 years to date him."

"You don't like her much do you?"

"She's your family and you're stuck with her. I dodge the requirement because she's my half-brother's half-sister. The guidelines don't apply when you're not related."

"I put the phone down on her. She probably won't speak to me for a week."

"Enjoy the peace while it lasts."

The car came to a stop near the spot where I'd seen the learner driver's near miss. I wondered how lonely my brother was that he'd persuaded his minders to venture out for this six-minute conversation.

"What else is news?" he said. "Any interviews lined up?"

"I have one." I replied. "I think I'll get it."

I didn't.

"I hope they don't ask for a reference."

They did. It's the reason I didn't get it.

To give you some idea of how close I came, please compare the following. I heard the following during my interview:

"The job was yours the second your CV landed on my desk. All that's left is formalities. We'll contact your previous employer for a reference."

I heard the following on my machine the next day:

"Ray, I'm sorry. We've been approached by a … a … a very strong candidate. It wasn't my intention to mislead you and we … that is, I … I mean we … we wish you every success in your job search."

I sat on my stairwell and my head sank into my hands for the brief moment between the end of the recording and the next message.

"Ray, it's Caitlyn. I'll meet you at our Italian, tomorrow at eight."

This will be a misunderstanding

When I had glimpses of hope, like Caitlyn agreeing to meet, a part of me thought my year had turned around. I don't remember feeling lucky. If I ever did, that changed the evening a car drove into my home.

I knew Gary Grey hated me. I knew Aaron Hayes hated me. Then a car parked in my living room and I knew life hated me too.

I lived in a tiny detached house at the bottom of a hill. My granddad called it Dead Sled Hill because the slope ran for 200 yards and if you rode a sled the length of it, you couldn't stop before you crossed the road at the bottom or hit the wall on the other side. My house was the other side of the road from the slope and behind that wall. The hill was steep enough that if you looked out of my window from the back of the living room, you couldn't see the sky, only the incline.

I can't tell you how many times I risked my life on that run as a child. It's amazing I was never injured, but I never once feared for the life of the house. I now consider this an oversight.

I was in an Italian restaurant when it happened. I was paranoid that my life's intermittent complications would interfere with my evening. My day passed without incident and I arrived early.

I stood up as Caitlyn approached the table. From the neck down, she looked amazing in a dress she knew I liked.

From the neck up, her face was a jumble of disappointment, resentment and stress.

I accepted the sign and prepared myself psychologically for the disastrous evening to follow.

"It's great to see you." I said.

It *was* great to see her. It also gave her the opportunity to tell me why it wasn't great to see me. I wanted to know as soon as possible.

"You're lucky I came at all." Caitlyn replied.

"What's wrong? You seem upset."

"Why would I be upset? Have you done anything to upset me? Did you forget to tell me something you thought I should know?"

"I'm sorry. I'm not sure what you're talking about."

We talked for ten minutes that seemed longer, during which Caitlyn provided additional criticism without any explanation.

The tense conversation ended when the restaurant's owner pointed two police officers in our direction. The officers confirmed my identity and showed me some IDs. As is my habit with all police badges, I checked their surnames for any indication that they might be among Gary's extensive network of uncles.

They told me that someone had tried to run Aaron Hayes off the road and invited me to discuss the incident with them further at the station. I understood why they suspected me. I'd wished him misfortune.

I stood up and put on my coat. Caitlyn looked at a menu unsympathetically.

"Not the reconciliation I had in mind." she said.

"This will be a misunderstanding. I'll call you."

"Don't bother."

Shortly after my arrival at the police station, all politeness disappeared. I antagonized the detectives accidentally when I didn't immediately acknowledge my involvement in all the crimes they thought I'd committed. I don't think their irritation was personal. My non-involvement represented a large amount of work for the people who would have to determine who was.

"You were at the restaurant thirty minutes early?" they asked, again, two hours into our conversation.

"Yes."

"The restaurant will confirm this?"

"Yes."

They'd asked me this five times already and I suspected they'd phoned the restaurant to confirm. They sighed deeply, I think because they believed me.

I looked up as a third police officer opened the door. He made his apologies for the interruption and asked me to confirm my address.

"There's another matter we need to speak about." he said without providing any details.

It seems to me that police officers have a number of skills and the ability to provide the minimum amount of information if they so wish appears to be one of them.

Fifteen minutes later, I climbed out of a police car, my eyes wide and my mouth open. I walked slowly towards the house I'd inherited from my grandfather.

In all the year's we'd walked to the top of the hill and taunted death by sledding back down it, we'd feared for our lives and done it anyway. I'd never once feared for the life of the house. It had stood for 100 years. It was made of sturdier materials than I was. I was never supposed to outlive it. I remembered all of this as I watched the firefighters retrieve the car from the front of it.

I didn't believe I was unlucky because I didn't believe in luck of any kind. I knew there had to be another explanation. I learned that reason thanks to a man called Sean Kidder.

One of life's inquisitive souls

On occasion, I share second-hand information. I can tell you of events I didn't witness and repeat words I didn't hear. I can't promise that my version is exactly how it happened, but I'm confident that it's close. I can say this because of Sean Kidder.

Sean is an investigator, a researcher, a scholar and so much more. He is one of life's inquisitive souls. If he hears the start of a story, he wants to know the middle and the end. Through a quirk of circumstance, he heard the start of my story. He looked into the rest of it and shared his findings with me.

He's my age, my height and my build. He is a fanatical Beatles fan and there is something of a post-Beatles John Lennon to his appearance that isn't a coincidence. I admit that there was a time when I didn't appreciate the way in which he arrived in my life without permission, but I've forgiven that now.

We met once towards the end of the year. We spoke for several hours and it was during this conversation that I received answers to questions that would have remained a mystery otherwise, such as how my house was destroyed.

As you might recall, it was a day I'd arranged to meet Caitlyn in Markden's best Italian restaurant. This is a figure of speech. It is Markden's only Italian restaurant, unless you count the supermarket's pasta aisle.

I was out all day and went straight to the restaurant. Caitlyn changed her plans last minute and went to my house. She hoped to meet me there, catch a ride and maybe drink without driving.

She shouted my name a few times and received no reply. She flicked through the mail, slipped a letter addressed to her into her bag and placed the others back on the side. She looked at the answering machine. There were 37 messages for the day, 33 more than we typically received.

She pressed play.

"Hi Ray. This is Caitlyn. I've remembered I want to check the post. Can we meet at the house? I hope you get this and aren't waiting at the restaurant."

I didn't get it. I was waiting at the restaurant.

Caitlyn reached out to press stop on the answering machine. She didn't reach it before the next message.

"Hi Ray. My name is Jenny. I have long blonde hair. I enjoy movies and dancing and …"

Caitlyn instinctively pressed skip and moved onto the next message.

"Hi. I'm calling for Ray. I'm Ali. I am 5 foot …"

Caitlyn pressed the skip button again and pressed it quicker with each successive message.

"Hi. This is Philippa …"

"Hello. My name is Susie …."

"Hi Ray. I'm Debbie …"

"Hello. I am …"

Caitlyn slammed the door as she left and she was still fuming when she reached the restaurant.

The same day, Gary stepped up his plans to kill me. Gary didn't know I'd lost my job, my company car and my company phone.

He parked near the office for the local paper. He spied on the location for some time and didn't see me for excellent reasons that he didn't determine. He had a black eye, a bruised face and a small chunk missing from a heavily bandaged foot. He also had a broken wrist, the origin of which I haven't explained yet.

From his old, battered wreck of a vehicle, he was close enough to see the cars come and go, but not close enough to identify each driver. He saw what used to be my company car pull to a halt in the reserved space nearest the entrance. He took out his notebook and dialled my old work number on his mobile. He didn't know he was watching and calling Aaron.

You may wonder how he obtained my work number given that it isn't in my interests to provide these details to someone with a history of violence and an interest in including me in an expression of that violence. The answer is I didn't. My mum did. I imagine the conversation went something like this.

"Gary, Roberta is seeing someone else. Let her move on."

"I don't want to."

"I know you're mad with Ray. Will you leave Roberta alone if I give you his phone number?"

"Oh. OK. That sounds fair."

Aaron answered my old mobile on the front steps of the office.

"Hello."

"Did you think I'd forget you?"

"Who is this?"

"I'm going to kill you."

Aaron disconnected the call and hurried inside the office. He cancelled his meetings and spent the day shaking in a corner. He thought through everyone that he knew who might wish him harm and decided that the anonymous caller was me.

At the end of a very unproductive day, he got into his car and plotted an alternative route home that nobody would expect. Gary caught up with him on a country road and accelerated until he could nudge Aaron's back bumper. He delivered a few more hits and then prepared to deliver a heavier blow.

Gary pressed the pedal to the floor and aimed for a collision as they neared a tight corner. Aaron, the worst driver I've ever met, on a route he didn't know, in a car he wasn't used to, swerved out of the way and disappeared through a fence. Gary accelerated into the newly vacant road and went straight on at the right turn.

Aaron guided his car across an uncomfortable half mile of field before crashing through another fence and returning to the main road. He went to the police station and told them I had tried to kill him.

By the time the police arrived at the scene of the accident, they found proof of Aaron's journey through the fence and no evidence of another driver. Gary was long gone, with a mild concussion and some whiplash to add to his growing list of injuries. His beaten-up car had suffered some new damage, but it was difficult to tell because the new damage blended seamlessly into the old damage.

Gary probably should have sought medical attention. Instead, in his mildly concussed state, he decided to finish what he'd started. He drove to my street, walked to my house and broke in. He was tired, hurt and wanted to complete our argument once and for all.

Aaron parked at the top of Dead Sled Hill. The hill sloped down from his position towards a row of houses, the most central of which was mine. He saw the car that had crashed into him pull to a halt near my home and a figure walk to my house. Aaron was close enough to see the cars pass my house, but he wasn't close enough to identify each driver. He didn't know he was watching Gary.

"It was you." he whispered.

It wasn't.

"I knew it was you." he whispered.

He really thought it was.

Meanwhile, Gary sneaked around my house and tried to select the best place for an ambush. The blow to his head affected his balance and the limp affected his stride. He collided with more furniture than he would have liked.

Aaron phoned the police, shared his new information and demanded my arrest. He weakened his case by describing my recent arrival at my house when the police knew I was sitting in one of their interview rooms. They also told him that they'd checked my alibi. They promised to continue their investigation.

"I know what I saw." he told them.

"If you release him, he'll try again." he told them.

The next day the police investigated the possibility that Aaron had invented his story to disguise another accident. It was consistent with his driving history and a theory that allowed them to abandon their search for another culprit. They also let slip their consideration of Aaron as the lead suspect in the death of my house. I added Aaron to the growing list of people interested in a world without me.

Meanwhile, Gary abandoned his plan for an ambush because he'd accidentally knocked over almost every item in the room. He sat on the sofa and waited for my return in the hope that I wanted a final confrontation as much as he did.

Aaron saw the shadow moving in the front room of the house. In need of a new plan, he looked around for inspiration. He saw an old abandoned car and glanced down the hill, following the journey it could take.

Gary heard a rumble of tires and the screech of out of control machinery. He looked out the window for an explanation and threw himself to the back of the room as the car crashed through the front window.

They pay my room service

As I mentioned earlier, I lived for several decades in a town called Markden. It's possible that you've never heard of it. It's probable that you'll never need to. It started as a village, grew into a small town and then faded into an afterthought as a suburb of the nearest city.

Most of that city's residents look down on Markden. We're not just any suburb; we're the least popular one. Growing up, we mocked the more prosperous parts of the city in retaliation, mostly because they mocked us first.

Despite the challenges of life in Markden, a struggling area that sits south of the city and outside of its ring road, all its children are taught that to move within the ring road is a betrayal. It's a claim that makes as much sense as Markden's pronunciation. After they demolished the remainder of my house and I sold the land for minimal profit, I betrayed my town. I moved inside the ring road and rented a small apartment in an area called Larkbridge.

I didn't know it at the time, but Caitlyn made the same move at the same time. She was unimpressed with the results of her new start. She added Markden to her list of disappointments and dismissed it from her future as she'd done to me a few months earlier. She thought a change in geography would provide the answers she needed.

My own motives were simpler. I needed work and my new apartment was closer to the available jobs. However, unlike Caitlyn, I knew a new location couldn't solve my problems. Larkbridge didn't belong to Ned Dwyer, but the man it belonged to wasn't much better and all the crooks ultimately report to the same group of criminals anyway.

In my corner of the world, if you break the law, you probably work for someone who works for someone who used to work for Brad Doyle. If you don't, you keep this to yourself. Being outside of Doyle's influence can be risky. Being his enemy can be fatal. Doyle is old. He's retired. He's still more dangerous than most people will ever be. My brother's outside of that control now.

My brother Warwick is a crook and he always has been. Don't judge him. I know his story and there's not much else he could have been. For most of his life, he worked for somebody who worked for somebody who used to work for Brad Doyle. In his case, Warwick worked for Ned Dwyer.

Brad Doyle is the stereotypical reformed gangster. He goes to the opera. He hosts dinner parties for local politicians, lawyers and doctors. He donates generously to local charities with only minimal publicity. He is in many ways the perfect citizen, but only if you ignore where all his wealth originated.

In almost all respects, Doyle successfully retired. He only stepped back into the spotlight when the police dragged him there.

The police saw him walk away and they weren't happy about the success of that walk. The reasons for their continued interest in his potential incarceration for something, anything, everything, were entirely personal. I think, if pushed, they would admit that. He took them on and won, and they don't like losing. They thought he should be in prison and every minute he wasn't upset them. He upset them a lot.

Doyle's former lieutenants, the ones who inherited his territory, are an interesting group too. There are seven of them. Though they are legally British, they all have parents who were born somewhere else. They're a kind of organized crime United Nations. There's an Irishman, an Egyptian, a Korean, a Russian, a Dane, a Jamaican and a Spaniard. Five of them look after a portion of Doyle's old territory, an area that includes both the town I'd abandoned and the town I'd adopted. The Dane looks after the money. The Russian is the one the others call when they need help with something.

The locals routinely reference the lieutenants by the country their parents called home. If someone talks about The Irishman or The Spaniard and doesn't provide context, everyone can fill in the blanks. If half the rumours are true, The Russian and his close-knit group are the worst. He's the one they say you never want to meet. It's poetic license. You don't want to meet any of them.

As we reached the end of February, Warwick was on their radar. Fortunately for my brother, they still considered him Dwyer's problem. As we got closer to the trial, we expected that to change, a potential problem for Warwick's nearest relative and his all-round favourite person, both of which are me.

I ignored that as a future crisis and focused on the opportunity to spend more time with my brother. It was in

March that we stopped meeting in cars and started meeting in hotel rooms.

During the visits, we escaped from our implausible lives by watching the fictional events of implausible TV shows. We watched a lot of television, often with Warwick's bodyguards hovering nearby. Sometimes his minders pretended to mind something. Mostly they watched the shows and helped eat the take-out food.

"Is Caitlyn returning your calls yet?" Warwick asked.

"She picked up this morning. She thanked me for the worst evening ever. I've met some of the idiots she's dated so that's an achievement. She still won't tell me why she was upset when she arrived at the restaurant."

"What are you going to do?"

"Right now? I'm going to change the subject. What else is news?"

"Ned's got a new errand boy."

"Anyone I know?"

"Darren Rourke."

"I know Darren. That's not a surprising career development."

I suspect every school has one. He's the boy who is shorter then he wants to be, weaker than he wants to be and less popular than he wants to be. He compensates by being crueller than everyone else is. He has a meaner streak, a shorter fuse and an eye for weakness. He has a capacity for targeting the few individuals who are shorter, weaker and less popular than he is.

In my school, he was called Darren Rourke.

Darren allied himself with the tallest and toughest boys. They somehow managed to befriend, begrudge and belittle him at the same time. He was pettier than they were and hated more than they were. He kidded himself that everyone's failure to retaliate wasn't due to the height of his allies.

As I remembered the highlights of Darren's school career, Warwick's news made more and more sense. I couldn't imagine Darren working for anyone other than Ned Dwyer.

"The thing to remember about Darren is that he's basically a coward." Warwick said. "That's what makes him dangerous. If you see him, talk tough. If you show weakness, he'll think he has you scared. You don't want to be the reason he makes a name for himself.

"I'll keep it in mind."

We each took a swig of beer and our eyes drifted towards the television.

"How do you watch this?"

"You see a few episodes and you get hooked. There must be subliminal messages or something."

I took another swig and turned back to face my brother.

"You were saying the trial might not be for six months."

"I'm a small part of a big investigation. They haven't even spoken to Ned yet."

"That's going to be a lot of moving around for you."

"Daytime TV and room service is better than prison."

"Don't take this the wrong way, but how did you qualify for witness protection? You're not exactly the top of the food chain."

"No one has said so, but I think that they think that if I testify against Ned, he'll cut a deal against Brad Doyle."

Warwick glanced at his minder's poker-face expression.

"That theory has a lot of guesses."

"I know, but it's the only way I can explain why they pay my room service. Have you seen how much I spend in room service?"

"I can guess."

"That reminds me. Have you eaten? I was thinking fried chicken."

Warwick glanced at his minder's Cheshire Cat grin.

A week later, I was in an interview. I liked my chances until my interviewer paused for a phone call. I know how conceited it sounds that I guessed the call was about me.

You'd understand my assumption if you'd seen the way he glanced at me during the conversation.

"Where was he seen? … And you're sure that's why he's here. … Thank you."

He put the phone down and smiled weakly for my benefit. It was a nice gesture.

"Ray, you're the best candidate."

"Why do I have the feeling I still won't get it?"

"It's not your qualifications or your past work."

"If it's about my references …"

"Aaron Hayes hates you. He hates me too. Aaron hating you is my favourite part of your application. I want to hire you and tell him myself what I've done."

"Then I don't see the problem."

"The problem is Ned Dwyer. We've heard you're unpopular with Ned and we can't risk his attention."

"It won't interfere with my work."

"I'm sorry. We're past that. One of his people is waiting outside for you. I'm told it's a man called Darren Rourke."

The understated version of dead

I left the building slowly and walked straight towards Darren. He was leaning casually against a car. He wore an old leather jacket that had seen better days. The jacket spoke of 100 adventures and countless fights. He'd bought it second hand.

I hadn't seen Darren in years. I'd imagined few changes in his personality or appearance. I'd pictured a slightly older, slightly taller, slightly meaner version of the teenager I'd known. I would have gone two for three. He wasn't any taller.

Further back, and out of the building's line of sight, were three more men. They were bigger than Darren was and ready to intervene if I tried anything. Clearly, Darren's approach to being a tough guy hadn't changed since our school days.

"Did you get it?" Darren asked.

Darren's knowledge of the interview meant that Ned had switched from his usual tactic of arranging my dismissal to ensuring that nobody hired me in the first place.

"Sadly, no." I replied.

"I hope my appearance didn't influence their decision."

"It did. But hey, my brother's trying to have you all imprisoned so you have your reasons. How's the new job going Darren?

"I'm enjoying it."

"Job security has to be a worry. I heard what happened to the guy you replaced."

"You know how rumours work. You probably heard the exaggerated version."

"I heard he's dead? What's the understated version of dead?"

"Oh, he's all dead. He died quicker than your brother will."

"Are you going to ask where Warwick is?"

"Where is Warwick?"

"I don't know."

"That's what I thought you'd say, but we looked for him, we got tired of looking. We decided, hey, there's no harm in asking."

"They're moving him around and keeping me in the dark. He might phone in a few weeks."

"You wouldn't lie to us?"

"I probably would. I don't need to."

"Tell him if he steps inside a courtroom, we'll kill everyone he ever cared about and we'll start with his little brother."

"I'll give him the message."

"You don't look scared. You should be."

"Darren, we both know you can't do anything without Ned saying so. Right now, we're having a polite conversation when constructing sentences isn't really your thing. You don't even have permission to call me mean names."

Darren leaned towards me and lowered his voice.

"Are you trying to make me look stupid?"

"Do you need help?"

Darren smiled and stood upright again.

"You have no idea how much I want your death on my conscience."

"You want to kill me? Go ask Ned for permission. Ask nicely."

"We'll see you real soon."

"Tell Ned my girlfriend left me. He likes to hear I'm doing well."

Darren walked away without replying.

"Talking tough?" I whispered to myself. "You better be right brother."

Somewhat indecisive on how he planned to kill me

After Sean Kidder decided to research me, he had the opportunity to meet Darren Rourke. His conclusion was that Darren isn't as dangerous as he thinks he is. I think that's a fair description.

Other than Darren's dishonest self-appraisal, the other factor working against him when he first re-entered my life was that he had to ask approval for everything. He was a new member of the team and he had the short leash to prove it. Darren wasn't allowed to be dangerous unless Ned agreed to it.

Gary should have been a bigger problem because he could act on every thought that entered his head. Fortunately for me, the thoughts that enter his head are a lower quality than the thoughts that enter everyone else's.

I didn't see as much of Gary in February as I was expecting. I later discovered that he spent most of the month recovering from an injury he'd suffered during an attempt I'd barely noticed. The accident went something like this.

Gary's uncle Trevor is a driving instructor. Gary borrowed his car without permission, confident he could return it before anyone noticed it was gone. It's a specially designed instructor car with a wheel and pedals for both seats so that the instructor can take control at any time. Gary opted to drive from the instructor's seat.

He tracked me down to Markden's high street and trailed me slowly in the congested traffic. The high street's traffic is always congested because the road isn't designed for today's volume of cars. He gained slowly.

Gary drove with his left hand on the steering wheel and his right hand on a gun. As the car drew level with me, he stretched his arm out of the window and didn't notice the approaching lamppost. His wrist struck the post. The gun dropped loudly and harmlessly into a litterbin. Gary pulled his hand back into the car and suppressed his scream. He drifted between the lanes and swerved out of the path of an oncoming bus.

I am told that he and his uncle no longer speak.

At the beginning of March, after he'd completed the minimum amount of recovery and recuperation, Gary went through a car-as-a-deadly-weapon phase. This typically involved attempts to run me over. However, he had injuries to his left foot and his right wrist that affected his driving. The significant drop in his steering ability didn't align well with the precision required to hit a moving target.

He eventually abandoned this phase after an attempt that saw him miss me and hit the top of the staircase that links the high street to the river pathway. He jumped from the vehicle three seconds before his journey took an unplanned, underwater detour.

I admit to some guilt in saying this, but watching his car bounce down 22 steps on its way towards the river is actually a happy memory.

The second half of March, he disappeared again. At the time, I assumed an absence due to self-injury, and perhaps caused by clumsiness, bad luck or both. Yet again, it was because of Sean Kidder that I heard the story, including the part played by Aaron.

Aaron Hayes was a psychological mess due to the phone call and the car accident. He spent a month awaiting the next attempt on his life. His nerves frayed beyond all recognition due to its failure to arrive. He still hadn't worked out how I had such a convincing alibi. He still hadn't considered the possibility that his attacker was somebody else.

Unable to handle another month of waiting for what he considered an inevitable assault, he decided his only available option was to kill me. This incidentally does appear to be the misguided and popular approach selected by many of the people I upset.

Aaron was somewhat indecisive on how he planned to kill me. He started to follow me and hoped what he observed might grant him some inspiration. He contemplated a car-as-a-deadly-weapon phase, presumably because he hadn't witnessed the experiences of the last person to contemplate one.

Meanwhile, Gary became a repeat customer for a man called King Rat. Despite his reputation as a man who can get you anything, his name has nothing to do with the novel or movie of the same name and everything to do with the fact that he looks like a rat. I don't mean this cruelly. If you met him, you'd draw the same conclusion. It's quite uncanny.

He owns an innocuous-looking shop in the middle of a housing estate. It's a fascinating treasure trove that sells everything you might need and almost everything you'll never need. The shop is a series of narrow pathways between floor-to-ceiling shelving units and a till situated strategically next to the only exit to dissuade shoplifting.

Gary entered the shop, his right arm heavily bandaged. He checked that he was the only customer and then they had a conversation that went something like this.

"I need a gun."

"I extend my sincerest greetings to you too. What happened to the last one?"

"I misplaced it."

"You misplaced it how?"

Gary started the story of how he hurt his wrist, and then thought better of it.

"It doesn't matter how. It only matters that I need another one."

"What kind do you need?"

"I need the kind that fires bullets. What do I care?"

"You'll care when you see the prices. Are you hoping to keep this one more than two weeks before you lose it?"

King Rat talks condescendingly to everyone this way. His shop is too useful in too many ways for him to prioritize customer service.

They talked models and capabilities and strengths and opinions before Gary settled on the cheapest weapon on offer. He went looking for me the second after he left the store.

He tracked me down to Markden's high street. He trailed me slowly in the congested traffic. All of Gary's attention focused on me as I ambled along the pavement. I didn't notice that the driver of the car over my shoulder was Gary. I didn't notice that the driver of the car behind him was Aaron. Gary didn't notice that the driver of the car behind him was a driver who was focused on me.

Gary struggled to drive because of the pain in his wrist. He took his left hand off the wheel and attempted to steer using his knees. He lifted his bottom off the seat and tried to draw the gun from the back of his trousers. He looked as the car in front stopped and he slammed on the brakes. Aaron's car shunted Gary's and Gary accidentally pulled the trigger.

The gun was in the back of his jeans.

Use your imagination.

In addition to being the incident that will forever dictate how Gary sits down, this was also the event that gave me some insight into Aaron's intentions for the months to follow. However, to his credit, Aaron managed to survive them without shooting himself. I admit it's a low bar, but it's a good one to clear.

In late March, I went back to work for a previous employer, the only one that would consider rehiring me. The job involved taking complaint calls on behalf of a large telecoms company. They hire almost anybody.

Working in a complaint department is a poorly paid, thankless task. In terms of abilities, it requires basic math, minimal communications skills, a thick skin and not much else.

As the recipient of the complaint, you represent the offending company the callers wish to criticise and slander. They say mean things. They use mean names. Most people can't handle the abuse and quit within six months. In my previous spell with the company, I lasted more than a year. I only left because Ned decided it was time.

You may wonder why I would apply to a company that previously asked me to leave.

1. I have the skill set and I can take the abuse because its tame compared to the other problems in my life.

2. They didn't fire me. They were nervous about their appalling dismissal rate and didn't want me to contribute to an already embarrassing statistic. I resigned at their

request instead. My immediate termination would have blocked my return. A voluntary resignation didn't.

3. The turnover at the company was high across all the departments. Nobody who knew the real reason for my resignation still worked there.

The only mark against my application was their suspicions. In the history of the company, no one had tried to return before. I could tell that troubled them. They hired me anyway. They hire almost anyone.

Outside of work, I met with Warwick whenever possible. He would send a car for me and we'd spend a few hours at his latest secret location. We'd watch television, eat take-out and discuss his latest philosophies.

During these months, he had a lot of time to think through life, the universe and everything. Much of what he concluded was nonsense, but it enlivened our conversations because I never knew what wisdom he would share with me next.

"I'm thinking about getting married." he said half-way through my visit.

I looked up from my meal. Of all the conversations he'd launched that afternoon, this was the most surprising.

"I didn't know you were seeing anyone?"

"I'm not, but I have a feeling there's someone beautiful out there for me."

"You seem pretty sure."

"The way I see it, men and women pair off in terms of eligibility, with only a few notable anomalies of bad taste and insanity. The stunning women are paired with stunning men, the good looking with the good looking, the average with the average, and so on. Eventually, you get the ugliest man and woman in the world falling in love and having ugly children. Are you with me so far?"

"I think so."

"But there are more women than men in the world. Therefore, if we presume that the proportions of each standard are comparable between genders, then there are beautiful women out there who have to settle for average men. I'm an average man. All I have to do is find one of these beautiful spare women."

"You have too much free time."

"Yes, I do, but I also have a lifetime of evidence. I don't know how many times I've seen a beautiful woman with a guy who doesn't deserve her, but you never see a great looking guy with an ugly woman. My Spare Women theory is the only explanation."

"You need to get out more."

"Yes, I do. Now I have my motivation. I need to find my spare woman. If I find two, you want one?"

"The only one for me is Caitlyn."

"She despises you more with each passing day."

He was right. She did. I had to admit that was a hurdle.

Increasingly complicated failure

During April, Gary went through what Sean Kidder dubbed a Wile E Coyote phase. Gary's line of thinking, which is flawed and difficult to defend, goes something like this:

"I am one of life's less intelligent specimens. I've tried and failed to achieve something using some of the simplest strategies available. I will now adopt increasingly complicated strategies in the hope that this will somehow bring me greater success."

It didn't work. It brought him increasingly complicated failure.

On a side note with only a tangential relationship to the story I want to share, I read somewhere that coyotes have a higher top speed than roadrunners. I still love the cartoon I saw as a child, but I have to admit that it lied to me.

All the coyote had to do to catch the roadrunner was run after him. Part of me is OK with that. As a child, I rooted for the coyote anyway. He was creative, inventive and funny. The roadrunner was smug and annoying.

Maybe I am overthinking this. Maybe the cartoon roadrunner is freakishly fast. Maybe the coyote continues to trust in Acme products because the fraudulent commercials repeatedly persuaded him. And maybe after all of my near-death experiences, I should be a little more sympathetic to the roadrunner.

Sorry. I'm digressing and I wanted to tell you the story of how Gary tried to drop a piano on my head.

Gary was working for one of his uncles. He does this a lot. The employment rarely lasts long, but that is OK because he has a lot of uncles.

Gary's Uncle Barry is in the moving business. His firm empties houses and they sometimes have the permission of the property's owner. On the occasions they don't, Gary's uncles in Markden's police force protect them.

In early April, Gary's uncle secured a legitimate contract from the old music school in Larkbridge to move all of their instruments to a small, purpose built college. Their existing location was a beautiful, stately building, among the oldest in the city. Its unquestionable beauty (in part due its age) was compromised by the likelihood that it might collapse (also due to its age).

This relocation was a delicate operation due to the value of each instrument, but it was well within the expertise of the moving firm. They have many years of experience, legal and otherwise. The only real issue was the piano.

The Old Man, as the school called it, was a full size grand piano. It was wider than every door in the building, including the one for the room it sat in. It was taller than every window in the building, including the ones for the room it sat in.

There is some debate as to how anyone got it into the room in the first place. Popular opinion is that the school's original owners lifted it into the second storey and built the room's outside wall afterwards. This theory was the inspiration for how Gary's uncle planned to retrieve it.

They partially removed the college's outside wall, a crime against a structure of such history and character if you disregarded its imminent demolition. They attached a rope to the piano, threaded the rope through a secured crane and planned to lower it out.

That was where I came in. I often walked past the music school because it was the quickest route to half a dozen places I visited regularly, including the bus and the train stations that were my means to get to the other half. I also liked it because it was a beautiful building and I loved the unpredictable bursts of live music that escaped from its open windows.

Gary had watched my movements and seen my patterns. He knew the routes I took and the times I took them. He knew I loved to walk past the music school and he had access to a very large piano. He saw potential in an accident that might cause my immediate and musical death.

His plan made a number of assumptions. It needed me to walk on that exact route at a specific time. It needed me to stay on the school side of the road and not vary my routine if I saw a group of workers moving heavy objects. It needed my failure to recognise one of the workers as someone with an established willingness to commit criminal acts that might affect my life expectancy. His entire plan relied upon a series of uncontrollable factors.

The laws of plausibility suggested that he couldn't position me under that piano. Yet, as unlikely as it sounds, he defied the odds. I walked into the trap exactly as he'd dreamed, and although I admit that I don't know that he'd dreamed about it, it isn't far-fetched to suggest that he did and in all its messy details.

I walked past the school that afternoon. I stayed on the school side pavement. I didn't recognize Gary beneath his baseball cap. I walked underneath an old and heavy piano. Gary released his rope. I imagine that he smiled as he did so.

His luck ran out.

The piano was very old and very heavy. Gary's uncle had realized it was too heavy for one rope. So, at some point between Gary devising his plan and the piano's flight from the building, the uncle decided to attach two additional ropes, one to support some of its weight and a second to help swing it out of the room. For reasons I can't confirm, other than an obvious comment on his intelligence, Gary failed to appreciate the significance of the additional ropes.

When Gary released his rope, three things happened:

1. Gary's uncle shouted Gary's name, presumably in the mistaken, momentary belief that this would persuade Gary to grab the discarded rope and resume his key role in sharing the instrument's weight.

2. Gary's uncle tugged on his rope violently to take some of the additional weight, maintaining its height and causing it to swing in his direction.

3. I noticed and recognized Gary due to the desperate screaming of Gary's uncle.

It was because of this third point that I had a perfect view of Gary's face and its resultant expression when the grand piano hit his uncle.

The uncle survived.

I am told that he no longer speaks to Gary.

It was during this same period that Gary stole a venomous python from an eccentric reptile collector (by which I mean that the collector is eccentric, the reptiles have fairly standard personalities for their species).

It was an ingenious heist whose perfect orchestration is at odds with its perpetrator's ability. Gary doubtless planned to abandon the creature in my home. Instead, he accidentally misplaced the snake in his rental apartment, an act of supreme stupidity that resolved the karmic imbalance of his earlier brilliance.

Gary was unable to locate it. For reasons I won't criticize, he was reluctant to look that hard. Instead, he switched to a spontaneous Plan B.

He moved.

He packed some belongings and abandoned anything in dark corners that might be home to a dozing reptile. He surrendered his damage deposit and neglected to tell his landlord of his departure.

Incidentally, Animal Services caught the happy, overweight snake in a basement six months later after an investigation into a reduction in rodent sightings.

You might have read about the on-going court case. The python's original owner sued for the return of his favourite pet. In addition to being a dangerous animal with an inexplicably unthreatening name (he's called Albert), the snake is also the principal beneficiary in his owner's will. The custody battle continues to this day.

To my knowledge, nobody has asked Albert what he wants. He was probably happiest living in a basement and resolving a local rodent problem.

Finally, I should tell you the story of how Gary accidentally triggered a turf war between two of Markden's teenage gangs.

Markden has so many gangs of insignificant membership numbers that very few of them are an issue, but they are a collective irritant. Two of the more infamous groups are known locally as The Kitts and The Durants. The former deny it, but I suspect they named themselves after the car from Knight Rider. The latter are named for a family of former members who started the original group, but ultimately quit gang life to start their own taxi business. Both gangs keep out of the way of the people who work for Ned Dwyer, a group known locally as People who work for Ned Dwyer.

A month before he tried to drop a piano on my head and two weeks before he stole Albert the python, Gary tried to set fire to my house in an amateurish attempt at arson. In a lapse of concentration, the likes of which has afflicted most of his adult life, he set fire to the wrong house. Thankfully, nobody was in it at the time.

I think what really confused him was that my house no longer existed. He'd benefitted from front row seats for its partial demolition, but he had somehow missed the newsflash that the rest of it hadn't lasted much longer. As such, he instigated the attack, unaware that I had already moved to a completely different neighbourhood.

The house he mistakenly picked belonged to the self-proclaimed leader of The Durants (the gang, not the family), a man who'd benefitted from the gang's adoption of self-proclamation as an electoral system after they'd run out of Durants (the family, not the gang).

The Durants suspected The Kitts. They threatened swift and violent retribution, although not so swift as to act prior to an extensive and increasingly violent series of retributive threats.

The city's gang liaison officer intervened (the city's gang liaison unit was an officer, not a department, because budget cuts had left them with insufficient funds to support more than one person's liaisons). He persuaded the Durants that it was a case of mistaken identity and not the first stage of a turf war. They backed down.

One of Gary's uncles in the police force, eager to exclude Gary from connection with the crime and possible retaliation, spread a rumour that the arson attack was the first stage in a turf war. The Durants believed the rumour and threatened swift and violent retribution, although it might only be considered swift when cross-referenced to the renewed interest in retaliation and not when considered against the original attack.

The gang liaison officer intervened. He spoke with the Durants and persuaded them that it was a mistake as he'd originally told them. With the additional information he'd obtained since their previous conversation, he provided them with a brief and unofficial description of Gary's attempt to hurt me and an explanation of the unsuccessful attempt. The Durants backed down.

The temporary calm lasted until one of the smarter members of The Durants noticed some implausible elements in the gang liaison officer's explanation, notably that the supposed and actual targets didn't share a house number, street name or housing style. The Durants decided that nobody would be so stupid as to attack a house that had almost nothing in common with the intended target. They reverted to their own theories of culprits and motives, and then threatened violent retribution. They wisely abandoned any mention of swiftness and nobody commented on the likely timeframe of any resultant violence.

The gang liaison officer intervened. He spoke with the Durants and persuaded them that it was a mistake as he'd originally told them. He conceded the implausibility of the perpetrator's mistakes and, with the additional information he'd obtained since their previous conversation, persuaded them that Gary was an idiot. They backed down.

One of Gary's uncles in the police force, eager to discredit any rumour that painted Gary as clueless and incompetent, spread a rumour that the arson attack was part of a turf war and contrary statements were the result of police corruption. As a result, an internal investigative unit reviewed the gang liaison officer's behaviour and his connections to the gangs with which he liaised. The liaison officer, disillusioned by the entire experience, retaliated with such a spirited defence that the internal investigative unit closed the review and recruited him.

The end of this particular tale is that the much-discussed retribution never occurred. All the threats reached the ears of senior police management and risked triggering a response that would complicate the business dealings for all of Markden's gangs, including Ned Dwyer's. Dwyer told both gangs to cut it out. They agreed. He's persuasive that way.

On a related note, the Durants (the family, not the gang), heard a rumour that The Kitts were targeting them. They blamed The Durants (the gang, not the family) for dragging them back into an argument that they'd tried hard to vacate. In retaliation, they burned down the new home of The Durants' self-proclaimed leader. Thankfully, nobody was in it. To this day, there is a feud between the Durant family and the Durant gang.

This story goes someway to explaining the local expression for how some of Markden's success stories are dragged back to the town they worked hard to escape. You can take a Durant out of Markden. You can't take Markden out of a Durant.

Persistent and occasionally humiliating rejections

Before I go on, I should tell you more about Caitlyn. If I don't, you might question why I cared so much about a reunion with someone so invested in not caring about me.

Caitlyn is the love of my life. I am intermittently the love of hers. Some of you might question whether you can be the love of someone's life for a period that is significantly less than a lifetime. I admit that's a fair question. I don't have a great answer.

You may have formed an early picture of Caitlyn based on our least successful year. It's possible your picture isn't accurate. I haven't told you about the time she nursed me to health after Ned's driver ambushed me. I haven't told you about the time she told a thug twice her weight to go through her if he wanted to hit me. I told you about the worst date we ever had and I haven't described the 100 best.

She is absolutely the love of my life. I may or may not be the love of hers, but there were definitely times when I believed I was. For most of last year, I believed it as much as ever. That's the only way I can explain why I wasn't discouraged by her persistent and occasionally humiliating rejections. It's the only way I can explain my excitement on the rare occasions she agreed to meet me.

In late April, I invited her to dinner at our favourite restaurant. To my surprise, she said yes. To my surprise, she showed up. My story might have taken a different turn if I'd showed up too.

At about the time that Caitlyn arrived at the restaurant, I was sprinting through the woods between Larkbridge and the ring road. About thirty feet behind me was Gary Grey, armed with yet another gun from King Rat. He was surprisingly fast and stubborn for a man who'd made a recent habit of firing bullets into parts of his own anatomy.

Suddenly the trees ended and I fell down a steep incline. I rolled head over heels into the middle of the road that cuts the forest in half. I heard the screeching of brakes and looked up in time to see the front bumper of an approaching car.

If you want to be glass half full about the situation, the car slowed down before it hit me.

The driver of the car climbed out hesitantly. She was a forty-something in designer clothes and designer sunglasses. The look went well with her expensive car. I noticed this as I lay on my back and contemplated the feasibility of short-term goals such as sitting up or moving limbs.

"That's a nice car." I said. "I'm really glad such a nice car hit me."

It's possible I'd hit my head.

"Are you OK?" she said.

"Am I OK? You hit me with your car."

"You ran out in front of me! What did you think you were doing?"

"I apologize for the damage I've done to your car. I feel bad about it. It's a very nice car."

It's possible I had a concussion.

She calmed from her initial, defensive response and kneeled alongside me.

"Can I help?"

She lifted me carefully to my feet. I was bruised, not broken.

"Honestly, I had no time to swerve."

"I know. I was just feeling sorry for myself."

"Do you need a hospital?"

"No. I think I'll be OK."

I wasn't OK. I needed a hospital.

"… Do you need a ride?"

I saw Gary Grey watching us from the top of the incline. I accepted her offer.

She was beautiful in many ways. She had great taste in clothing and enough money to buy from expensive stores. She drove a beautiful car and did so confidently, expertly, as if she belonged behind its wheel. She had obvious class, and I don't mean perfect Queen's English and an education at an exclusive school, although she definitely had the former and I suspect the latter too. I mean there was a quality there, immediately apparent, immediately impressive. The only flaw to her, the only flaw at all, was the bruising to her face.

I didn't notice it at first. It was driver's side and hidden from the passenger seat until she turned her whole head to face me. She didn't do this until several minutes into our journey. I spontaneously made some assumptions about her husband, of whom a wedding ring suggested existence. As it turns out, my assumptions were close.

Shortly after this, I noticed the suitcases on the back seat.

"New house?"

"New life."

"I'm sorry."

"Don't be. I'm the fool who married the wrong man. He's changed a lot since then and he won't take my decision well. I'm scared what he might do when he finds my note."

"If that's the type of man he is, you're making the right choice."

"Thank you. You don't know how good it is to hear someone else say it. How about you? What are you running from?"

"My sister's ex-boyfriend. She asked for my opinion. I shared it. They broke up. He blames me."

"He's trying to hurt you?"

"He's trying. I'm happy to say that he isn't very good at it. You can drop me anywhere here."

"Are you sure you don't want the hospital?"

"No, there's somewhere I need to be and I haven't much time."

She pulled over next to Markden's Italian restaurant and I climbed out.

"What's your name?"

"Ray."

"My name is Zara. You seem like a nice guy Ray."

"I try to be."

"Then I wish you luck… but don't run into any more roads."

I happily accepted her advice.

During the year, I had the opportunity to meet many interesting people in interesting circumstances. Zara was one of the nicest. Yes, she hit me with her car, but unlike the other people who have hit me with their cars over the years, she didn't intend to. For this reason and others, I am very fond of her.

I looked around the restaurant, but I couldn't see Caitlyn. I looked down at my watch as one of the waiters approached me. The staff know me because I'm a regular and because I memorably departed from my previous visit in a police car.

"She left a few minutes ago."

"Did she leave a message?" I asked.

"Yes, but I don't use that kind of language."

I would like to offer some advice to those of you who crave fame. I politely suggest that you crave money, success, happiness or a combination of the three. Fame is overrated and I say that as someone who achieved some and would have preferred less. I assure you that fame is less fun that you think it is.

After his departure from the publication that created him, Mal McCall enjoyed a high-profile re-launch as a columnist for a national newspaper. However, his reinvention was not a success. His new owners planned for publicity and received it. They planned for controversy and received it. They planned for popularity and accidentally created the most despised journalist in the country.

When I wrote as Mal McCall, I started each column with the words 'The Problem With' and followed these words with an aspect of our lives. It was a thinly veiled jab by a local at the locals based on local knowledge. I was part of the joke. I was a victim of my own commentary.

The new Mal McCall writers didn't take this approach. They attacked a section of society with a venomous swipe at their targets of the day. They weren't part of the joke. They weren't their own victims. It read as criticism instead of self-deprecation. It was vicious. It was contentious. It wasn't funny.

In the first two weeks alone, Mal McCall offended students, dog owners, musicians, the homeless, single parents, farmers, tradesmen, Christians, dentists and the Welsh.

Mal McCall was systematically offending every person in Western Europe other than white, male, twenty-something journalists who live in fashionable parts of London. He was the last person in the world I wanted to be mistaken for. Unfortunately, the online website that led the charge for his admonishment and immediate punishment used my picture as the face for the fictional Mal McCall. They got the picture from my mum.

In her defence, I will concede that my mother rarely causes my problems. However, when they cross her path, she is incredibly gifted at complicating them and magnifying their consequences. This is how it happened.

Mal's paper had wisely refused to co-operate with providing the names of the column's contributing writers. In response, the persistent and angry website tracked the origins of the column to Markden, to my old paper and eventually to my mum. They told her that I'd upset them. She told them I'd upset her too. They bonded over cups of tea and she let them take a photograph from the cabinet.

It's now the picture of choice for the assorted online discussions of Mal's various crimes.

The website labelled me as the creator of Mal McCall and gave me credit for some of his earlier work. It didn't caution that I hadn't written any of the recent, controversial columns. The rival newspapers picked up on the story as a consequence of their collective joy with the misfiring column. They neglected any explanation of my role and identified me as Mal McCall. My creation and I became synonymous in the psyche of his enemies, whether I liked it or not, and his unpopularity increased with each passing day.

I dreaded reading his column, but I had to if I wanted to know which segment of society would hate me exponentially more than the day before. Then in May, he exceeded my already considerable expectations of the hostile backlash he could provoke.

I walked to the newsagents, a regular part of my daily routine. I found my picture on the front page of a tabloid alongside a headline that asked if I was the nastiest man in Britain. The other customers were staring at me with fury and disgust. I paid and left quickly.

I didn't read the article when I got home. I knew the article's targets would be upset with me, but I was more concerned that the victims of every previous article had discovered what I looked like. As this represented such a high percentage of the population, I lost interest in protecting myself from that day's victims only.

I was about to leave for an important appointment when the phone rang. I assumed it was bad news, as most of the incoming calls were, and I hesitated. I wanted to believe that if I didn't answer it, the bad news wouldn't happen. It's an indefensible theory, but it seemed like a good idea for the few seconds I considered it.

I picked up after the sixth ring.

"Ray, it's Warwick. I'm glad I caught you. Have you got plans?"

"Caitlyn's agreed to meet for lunch."

"Really? That's great news. Congratulations. You need to cancel."

"Cancel? No. It's taken me weeks to persuade her."

"Ray, it's not safe. Did you read Mal's column today?"

"Not yet. What did he write?"

"Ray, he wrote about women. He wrote about the problem with women."

My immediate instinct was to swear. My subsequent instinct was to keep swearing. My resultant instinct was that there might not be a suitable time to stop.

We were advised of your situation

I took a bus from Larkbridge to Markden. During the short and memorable journey, I attracted a considerable amount of attention. I've attracted hateful stares before, but rarely in the volume that I witnessed that day. I also received under the breath comments from almost every woman who saw me.

The only exception was one of my fellow passengers. I noticed her because she was slight, pretty and blonde, but mostly because she didn't have homicidal rage written on her face. She had a haircut that was one part Tinker Bell and one part punk rock. She wore jeans and a jacket that hinted she was tougher than she looked. She glanced straight at me and then quickly away.

More typical was the woman who approached me at speed as I stepped off the bus. She slapped me and suggested that my family were ashamed of me (which is mostly true, but a lucky guess on her part).

Another example was the lady who punched me three times in the shoulder, paused, considered my crime, pondered her response, and then struck me again. I'm guessing a line of reasoning that determined I had committed a four-punch crime and not three as she'd originally suspected.

It was shortly after the latter that a schoolgirl kicked me in the shins. I heard her confess to her friends that she didn't know who I was, but she'd seen the other attacks and assumed I deserved it.

Later that day, I decided to grow a beard. It was time to look less like my least favourite journalist.

None of last year's dates with Caitlyn went to plan. They all went wrong in some fashion, but we varied the amount of time between our arrival and the date's degeneration beyond recognition. My meal with Caitlyn that day was the most successful of our bad dates in that we both enjoyed its first nine minutes. The average is somewhere around the three minute mark.

Caitlyn and I were at a table for two. Caitlyn appeared relaxed. She was smiling. Our topics of conversation hadn't progressed as far as mistakes, blame and name-calling. Then she noticed something that distracted her.

"We're being watched."

"I've been having this problem all day." I said. "There are people who think I write Mal McCall's new column. You wouldn't believe what he wrote today."

"I read it. You were brave to leave your apartment."

"Accept it as a compliment. Lunch with you was the only thing I'd risk it for."

"Complement accepted. Thank you."

She smiled again and tried to return to her menu.

"Ray, I'm sorry. I can't do this with her looking over every ten seconds."

I turned around and saw the pretty blonde from the bus, three tables away. We tried to ignore her without success for a few more minutes and I foolishly allowed Caitlyn's mood to deteriorate while I considered alternatives. By the time I walked over and sat opposite the blonde, the date was another irredeemable disaster.

"I think I saw you on the bus earlier."

"Yes, that may have been me." she replied.

Her accent was American, but other than ruling out Texas, Louisiana and Brooklyn, I couldn't be more specific.

"Why are you following me?"

"My name is Audrey White. I work for the United States government as a security advisor."

"That must be fun for you. Why are you following me?"

"I'm researching the effectiveness of spontaneous, improvised responses to on-going and varied acts of violence. I'm writing a paper on the subject."

"That's very interesting. Why are you following me?"

"We were advised of your situation and believe we can use your attempts at self-preservation as the basis for the research."

"What do you mean? What situation?"

"I mean that people try to kill you. I've been watching you for a while and the reports are true. It happens *a lot*."

I couldn't dispute that. It had been a busy week.

"But I don't want you following me."

"It actually works better if I don't have your permission because psychologically you won't make special exception for my presence."

"It works better if … you won't … What?"

"But I have been promised full cooperation by your government."

She took a copy of a legal document from her handbag and presented it to me.

"I don't believe this. You have government-approved access to stalk me. … It looks like I don't get a say in this, but could you at least back off at certain, pre-arranged times?"

"The terms of my assignment don't allow me to back off."

"Really? … What did you say your name was?"

"Audrey."

"Audrey, I'm appealing to your good nature and I'm asking nicely, which under the circumstances is very decent of me. … I'm on a date and you're killing it."

"I see. I'll try and be more discreet."

"Thank you."

I returned to my table.

"What's going on?" Caitlyn asked me.

"Life hates me."

My efforts at self-preservation

I decided to stay home. I wanted to give my face a break from the inevitable violence I would encounter if I ventured out. In response to my attempts to avoid trouble, my life discovered new ways to pursue its downward spiral.

If this were a movie, there would now be a montage of my incredulous responses to the surprising and dispiriting phone messages I took that week.

1. "He spoke to you when?"

2. "He accused me of what?"

3. "You got my number where?"

When I finally braved the streets, it was armed with some facial hair that reduced, but didn't end, the violence against me. I saw Audrey within minutes.

I went window-shopping in the hope that imaginary spending would distract me from my worries. Audrey stayed fifty feet behind me and turned to look in a shop whenever I did, regardless of which window this gave her. Eventually, her repetition of my movements became distracting. I humoured her feigned consideration of Cornish pasties and craft supplies. I abandoned our charade after her fake interest in pensioner's mobility vehicles. I stood silently alongside her until she reluctantly acknowledged my presence.

"I tried to be more discreet, as you requested." she said. "Each time I did, you attempted to lose me. So, I've returned to a more obvious presence."

"I didn't see you last night when Gary attacked me."

"I was watching."

A female passer-by spat a short comment as she walked past.

"You're a disgrace." she told me.

"Thank you." I replied and then continued my conversation with Audrey without pausing.

"You were watching? Did it occur to you I might need some help?"

"The terms of my assignment don't allow me to help."

"You're disgusting." a passing stranger told me.

"Thank you." I replied.

The insults bounced off me. I'd quickly developed the skill of acknowledging each slander without actually registering it.

"Oh, that's right. Helping me would invalidate your research."

"I appreciate your understanding."

"You appreciate my ... Stop being so polite! You're a nuisance. You're irritating as hell. Politeness isn't in the job description."

"I'm restricted by the terms of my assignment, but I'm trying to compensate for my intrusiveness. I could try and be less polite, if that was what you ..."

"Forget it. Please, forget it. ... But tell me one thing. The American government sent you here, right? How do they even know about me?"

I applied for permission to see my brother. I applied for permission to take Audrey with me. I don't think it's a coincidence that I got permission for both faster than I'd previously received for the first request only.

Warwick was perched on a bed in his hotel room, predictably opposite the TV. He turned the sound down as I entered. I remained standing.

"Is there a problem?" Warwick asked.

"Have you been trying to help me?"

"Is this about Caitlyn?"

"Did you phone her and tell her she was an idiot?"

"You're a great guy. I told her she'd made a mistake."

"You told her she was clinically stupid."

"I was hoping she'd change her mind about you."

"Did you sign me up to a dating agency?"

"You seemed lonely."

"Did you sign me up to a dating agency twice?"

"I reckoned that if Caitlyn didn't wise up, it'd be good for you to get out there again."

"You gave both agencies my phone number."

"That's for their records. It's not as if they give it to their clients. Why? Did you get some calls?"

I let out a short, sharp laugh.

"Is this why you wanted to talk?"

"Did you phone Aaron Hayes?"

"I asked him to leave you alone."

"You told him you'd hospitalize him. You forgot to say who you were and we sound alike on the phone. He reported me to the police."

"Sorry. Next time I'll leave a name."

"Don't phone Aaron. Don't phone Caitlyn. Stop trying to help me."

"Watch that tone, little brother. I've brought some trouble your way, and I feel bad about that, but if you think I'm at fault for everything going wrong in your life, remember there are four people who want you dead and I'm only to blame for two of them."

"Is that your best defence?"

"It sounded better in my head." he mumbled.

"Written to America recently?"

"Yeah. I saw this TV show and ... How did you know about that?"

"We're getting there. You were watching TV ..."

"They interviewed the senator of some obscure American state. He was complaining because he's had two attempts on his life this year. Two! I've had more than two this year. You had more than two last Tuesday! So I told him to stop complaining."

"You wrote to the senator of an obscure American state and told him he was a sad, pathetic drama queen."

"It was a slow day."

"You're in witness protection! Every day is a slow day!"

Audrey entered behind me, accompanied and watched closely by Warwick's bodyguards. Warwick's eyes widened. I've never experienced love at first sight, but thanks to these few seconds, I've witnessed it.

"Who's this?" he said, immediately smitten.

"The senator you wrote to doesn't believe you exist." I explained. "He thinks the letter was a political stunt from a British government critical of his isolationist foreign policy views. He's made a diplomatic complaint. The British government don't care because they don't like him and they think the letter was pretty funny. However, the Americans were interested in what you said about me."

I gestured to Audrey.

"They've commissioned an agent, *with* the permission of the British government, to monitor my efforts at self-preservation."

"They've done what?"

"You heard it right first time. Warwick, stop trying to help me."

Try to keep the lies consistent

After a few more weeks, Audrey dropped all the subtler aspects of her approach, few of which worked. For example, if I ate in a restaurant, she took the table next to mine instead of hiding in a corner. We would sit with our backs to each other, close enough that we could hear whatever the other person whispered into their menu. Our routine became seamless and it stopped troubling me that she was always there.

Courtesy of her decision to tail me everywhere, I introduced her to The Village Idiot. I arrived early enough to take one of the booths and I watched the room using the mirrors behind the bar. Audrey took the next booth over. More than fifty people arrived during the next hour and restricted my view of the entrance.

"When you get mad with Warwick, how long do you stay mad with him?" she said to her menu, in the spirit of our new communication strategy.

"I aim for a week. It's usually a day."

"You love him a lot."

"He's the only member of my family I like and I owe him for how he looked out for me as a kid."

From a distance, it looked like we were talking to ourselves and equally insane.

"Your brother has done some really dumb things." Audrey said. "He told me some of his stories and it's a miracle his life isn't worse than it is. It's a wonder yours isn't worse by association."

"I know."

She sighed deeply enough that I knew her next question would say more about her life than mine.

"Do you ever wish you had a different brother?"

"No, I don't, and I never will."

She didn't say any more. Ever since this discussion, I've assumed she has older siblings. The conversation also raised questions about when she'd heard my brother's stories. I suspected she'd added Warwick as a source for her research into my life and I could guess why he'd agreed to it.

"Is Aaron still back there?" I said.

Aaron Hayes had followed me here and taken a seat at the bar.

"Do you think he thinks you haven't seen him?" Audrey replied.

"I think he thinks that, yes."

"Word is that Aaron has been asking questions about you."

"What kind of questions?"

"He spied on the Italian restaurant in Markden, hoping you'd show. He saw you get out of an expensive car. He noted the plate and tried to trace the owner. I think he's hoping to work around your perfect alibi and identify your associates."

"That won't take him long. I don't have many associates left."

We both drank from our half-empty beer bottles.

"I almost feel bad for him." she said. "Should we send him a drink?"

"No. Let him feel he's doing well. Can I ask you some questions? If we're going to keep almost spending time together, I'd like to know you a little more."

"You can ask."

"Will you tell the truth?"

"No, but I'll try to keep the lies consistent."

I accepted her offer. It was as fair as she was likely to offer.

"Is your real name Audrey or is that part of your cover?"

She paused before replying.

"My mum liked Roman Holiday."

I liked her answer. I still don't know if it's true.

I saw Darren Rourke's reflection in the bar's mirror. As previous, three henchmen flanked him. This was the pattern for the months to follow. He always brought back up in the form of three associates. The men changed. The general descriptions didn't.

1. One was tall enough to be a professional basketball player.

2. One was big enough to lift a professional basketball player.

3. One was ugly enough to scare a professional basketball player.

Every set of three met these basic descriptions. It can't be a coincidence. Maybe it's Darren's unofficial recruitment policy. Maybe he read it is an industry best practice in Criminal Underlings for Dummies.

"Does he know you're here?" Audrey asked.

"I don't know. He's looking for someone though."

"I thought he didn't have permission to hurt you."

"The last I heard, he didn't. Are you committed to the non-interference rule?"

"It's against the terms of my assignment. If I interfere, it would invalidate the research. That's why I haven't mentioned that Gary Grey sneaked in with a large group two minutes ago."

"Right, because that would help me."

"Exactly."

Darren and his friends walked to the bar and took some seats. The customers nearest to them moved away and gave them space they wanted and hadn't requested. The barman placed some free beers in front of them. There was nothing in their actions or demeanour to suggest they were here for me.

I scanned the room and tried to determine my options. Audrey did the same.

"So, only two people trying to kill you tonight then?" she said.

"That would be my count. Maybe you should start making notes."

"Good luck."

"Thank you."

Audrey left her booth and took one of the newly vacant stools next to Darren. She took out her pen and paper.

I put on my jacket and plotted a route through the crowd to the main entrance. I suspected Aaron saw my intent. I knew Gary had. I looked at both men, took a breath and prepared to run.

A man sat in the seat opposite me. I assumed he'd seen my imminent departure and aggressively claimed the booth. He was forty-plus in age and wore an expensive suit on a body shaped like a bouncer's.

"We need to talk." he said.

"I was just leaving."

"I don't think so."

He took a gun from his pocket and placed it on his lap under the table. I glanced over at Audrey and she looked as confused as I was.

"Where's my wife?" he said.

"I don't know. Who is your wife?"

"Don't play stupid. It would be your last mistake."

"No, I suspect I'm destined to make a lot more."

He looked like a stereotypical Russian thug. I say this based on the portrayal of the aforementioned nationality and profession as presented by Hollywood movies. The similarity isn't coincidental. I later discovered that the man opposite me was a successful executive who found it professionally helpful to look like a dangerous criminal.

I assumed that he succeeded in mimicking this look because he had seen some of the same movies I had. I later discovered that he modelled his image on actual Russian thugs that he has dealt with over the years and they in turn base their image on the stereotype as portrayed in Hollywood movies because they find it influential when dealing with English executives.

"Where is she?" he repeated.

"I know you think I'm stalling but … Who are you?"

"My name is Grant Mahon. I know she left me for you."

"I think you've got the wrong guy."

"You were seen getting out of her car the day she left me."

I suddenly realized his identity.

"Zara?"

He nodded.

"I was hitchhiking. She gave me a ride. We had a short conversation and then I got out. I haven't seen her since."

"I don't believe you. And that's going to be a problem."

He said problem. His expression told me he'd already thought ahead to a solution I wouldn't like.

I've learned since this conversation that Grant Mahon, the man Zara fled from, is a force of nature. He is intense. He is relentless. He rarely loses. His business operates on a fine line between legal and deeply unethical.

His only brush with illegality is his weakness for hitting women. This isn't because he is intense. This isn't because he looks like a criminal or because he hates to lose. It's because he's a deeply unpleasant human being who deserves bad days until the one on which he dies.

The more I learned about Mahon, the more I understood why Zara left him. The more I learned about him, the happier I was that he couldn't find her. Most of that came after I'd worked out who he was.

I saw Gary Grey edging in my direction. I must have turned my head slightly because Mahon immediately took offence.

"I don't think I have your attention."

"No, you have it." I answered. "And you deserve it because you don't like me much. But I don't know where she is and I don't care what you believe and the man approaching the table likes me even less than you do.

I stood up and yelled "*He's got a gun!*" in a loud and overly theatrical manner.

Gary slipped in the confusion as 70 people ran for the door. I estimate that at least 20 of them stepped on him. I was first out of the exit and Aaron and Grant found their route to me blocked by the exodus.

By the time Grant scanned the car park, I was nowhere in sight. In frustration, he turned and punched the face of the person closest to him, which happened to be Aaron. I was ten feet away, cowering behind a car.

The next time we spoke, Audrey told me that she'd captured some good insights from the incident. She was sincerely grateful, which was never good news. Her gratitude usually followed an unwelcome meeting between my life and physical violence.

I found out later that Ned had sent Darren to put me in the hospital. He'd received disappointing news and I'm his go-to guy when he wants to finish a bad day on a good note.

A suitable alternative to my untimely demise

In May, the police briefly arrested me on suspicion of dishonestly and illegally persuading others to part with their money.

After the failure of April's attempts to kill me, Gary Grey had concluded that my lengthy incarceration would be a suitable alternative to my untimely demise. He decided to implicate me in some crimes. More specifically, he decided to implicate me in the crimes committed by his Uncle Ted.

Ted is a con man. He performs this work using false names and Gary persuaded him to use a pseudonym of Ray Knott. His uncle agreed because it was the kind of name he liked to use, sufficiently uncommon and yet simultaneously boring. Gary forgot to mention why he selected this particular name.

Unfortunately for Gary, he didn't think through several parts of his plan.

1. My dad was Jack Ray. My step-dad is Jack Knott. Gary combined these and got confused. Despite his obsession with me, he apparently didn't know my real name.

2. As I understand it, the majority of con men do not use their own name when they defraud people. For this reason, when investigating criminal acts of persuading others to part with their money, it isn't an automatic leap for the police to arrest everyone with that name.

3. I don't look anything like Gary's uncle. We are a different height, weight, shape, size and age. When the police questioned me, for no reason other than my name's similarity to that of the perpetrator, each victim told the police I was innocent.

I know a little about con men because they count my stepfather among their number and my stepfather counts me among his victims. Please don't dwell on that confession too long. He's in prison again and he'll be there for the next four years. Pretend he doesn't exist. That's what I do.

Given the above family history, you would forgive me for suspecting my stepfather's involvement in the false accusations. However, given my belief that only Gary would try to frame me for a crime and then proceed to get my name wrong, I suggested to the police that they consider a culprit from Gary's family tree.

Needless to say, Uncle Ted's brothers immediately quashed that line of enquiry and then warned him to change his temporary pseudonym. This alerted Ted to what Gary had attempted. I am told they no longer speak.

However, this tale leads nicely into some stories about Gary's extended family, a fascinating collection of miscreants, misfits, troublemakers and police officers.

Gary's mother has eight older brothers. Gary's father has seven older brothers. His mother's brothers really love their little sister. His father's brothers really love their brother's wife and each of them would love to be more than a brother-in-law. For many years, Gary's uncles looked out for him. Some of them competed for who would look out for him the most.

If you are curious, their names are Don, Dom, Des and Den, Ted, Fred, Jud and Sid, Mick, Mac, Rick and Malc, Larry, Barry and Trevor. I could tell you which side of the family each resides on, but to be honest, it rarely mattered. They tried to be his friend. He tried to be my enemy. By default, they became my half-hearted enemies. Some of them, notably the police officers based in Markden, caused me problems.

My favourite character among Gary's extended family is Uncle Sid, the amateur inventor. He can build anything and he likes a challenge. Gary persuaded him to build a giant catapult. Gary planned to launch something large, perhaps a dishwasher, presumably in the hope of crushing me.

After its manufacture, Gary organised a testing phase on some waste ground outside of town. He wanted to establish the distances that disused kitchen appliances would travel. On the first attempt, he used a fridge freezer, overloaded the catapult, fired himself backwards and flew through the windscreen of his own car. To this day, there are crash investigators confused as to how Gary's stationary vehicle ran him over.

Sorry. I'm digressing and I wanted to tell you the story of how Gary's uncles caught a serial killer.

One of Gary's uncles is a brilliant detective. One of Gary's uncles is a famous detective. In an ideal world, they would be the same person. Inconveniently, that isn't the case.

Gary's Uncle Mick is an investigator based out of the police force's regional headquarters. He takes his job very seriously, which is why he has never attempted to cover for Gary like some of his sister-in-law's brothers. He is excellent at what he does, a trait he shares with very few of his relatives. During a distinguished career, his investigations have convicted 23 murderers. It's unlikely you have heard of any of these 23.

Gary's Uncle Malcolm is an amateur sleuth. He's famous for the only two mysteries he ever solved, Skylight and Valentine. You may have heard of both because of the media coverage they received. As such, in most circles, Mick is less famous than Malc, despite the 23 to 2 score line.

I know very little of what follows. However, this is my best guess as to how Gary's Uncle Malc, an otherwise unexceptional fellow, captured two incredibly dangerous men.

Mick was working on a case involving three suspicious deaths that he was convinced had a connection. Nobody, including his colleagues, shared his fascination with the similarities. Mick's superior told him that the case needed a new direction and some new input.

Mick pretended to follow their advice. He invented a Cracker-style criminal psychologist and persuaded

Malcolm, his brother's wife's brother, to play the role. He neglected to tell anyone that they were vaguely related. He also forgot to mention that Malc's background wasn't in criminal psychology.

Malc came in and impressed everyone with insight into the case that he wasn't supposed to know and that Mick had secretly fed him. Then, after he'd demonstrated the brilliance of his instinctive deductions, Malc jumped to conclusions that Mick had provided and that Mick couldn't prove. Everyone credited it as genius.

When Mick jumped to conclusions, his bosses criticized him for breaking procedures. When Malc jumped to the same conclusions, Mick's bosses feted Malc as a modern-day Sherlock Holmes.

Malc suggested that the police look at the third victim's husband. They brought him in on Malcolm's recommendation and the killer caved under questioning. The press eventually dubbed the murderer Skylight after the rooftop windows he bypassed to enter houses. It was the same similarity Mick had noticed and his colleagues had ignored.

When Malc received all of the credit, Mick didn't care. He didn't solve cases for the prestige. He started to care when Malc changed their agreement.

The arrangement between Mick and Malc was supposed to be a one-time deal, but Malc enjoyed the praise. He offered to continue providing assistance. In response,

Mick's supervisors pressured Mick to involve Malc every time Mick didn't solve a case immediately.

Malc had below-average intelligence and depended completely on the tips that Mick provided. If one of Mick's cases hit a roadblock that stalled the investigation, Malc was the last person able to provide new ideas because all of his best ideas were Mick's. However, Mick couldn't reveal Malc's secret without embarrassing himself, damaging his reputation and risking his 23 convictions. Mick was stuck with a stupid sidekick as an unhelpful accomplice.

It was during this period that Gary persuaded his Uncle Malc to implicate me in some crimes. Malc, whose input into cases was largely fictional anyway, didn't see the harm if his fiction pointed the police in my direction.

There was never anything too specific. Malc would suggest someone who fitted my description or career path or hobbies or approximate address. During the month of June, the police questioned me regarding three separate murders. Malc thought he was helping his nephew and didn't see the harm in distracting the investigations. Mick saw the harm and he was furious.

Then, Mick transferred to another case. The press called the killer Valentine after the anonymous love notes he sent to his future victims. Mick was desperate to catch him. At the same time, Malc was desperate to repair his flagging reputation. The problem was that Malc's increasingly bizarre suggestions undermined the investigation. Any leads that Mick planned to pursue were shelved if they disagreed with Malc's theories and Gary was behind the scenes influencing Malc's theories.

Mick asked his superiors to pull Malc from the case. They pulled Mick instead and gave Malc a new team. With Mick out of the way, Malc finally obtained something he had always wanted and that Mick had always blocked. He wanted a press conference.

Malc believed that appearing to a wider audience was the best way to enhance his star status. Mick believed that Malc appearing to a wider audience increased the risk that somebody would detect the hoax. In the end, Malc was right, though not for the reasons that either of them predicted.

The strange, sprawling and confused press conference was a major success in two ways. Firstly, it established to Malc's legion of fans that he was too eccentric and perhaps too brilliant for mere mortals to understand. Secondly, its central premise that Malc's genius for capturing killers guaranteed the capture of the killer captured the attention of the killer who vowed to kill him.

Strictly speaking, Malc never solved the case of Valentine. However, due to this unexpected twist, he did capture him.

Valentine arrived on Malc's doorstep in the guise of a parcel deliveryman. It was an easy role for him to mimic because Valentine had a part time job as a parcel deliveryman. It was how he'd met his victims and targets.

He presented Malc with a padded envelope and asked him to sign for it. Malc invited him out of the torrential rain and into the hallway of his small, back-to-back terrace. Malc went to his kitchen in search of a pen. The door was closed and the deliveryman missing when Malc returned.

He ripped open the package and took out a valentine's card. Malc, the renowned master detective, took a few seconds to appreciate the card's significance. He took a few seconds more to realise that Valentine was probably in his house.

He walked slowly to the kitchen, retracing the steps he'd taken for the pen, confident that this was the one route he could trust. He opened a cupboard and took out a present from his brother Sid. It was a knife block with springs built in to each slot. The springs were supposed to release each knife at the touch of a handle. However, if improperly used, it launched knives dangerously across the room and this was why he'd stored it safely in the back of a cupboard.

Malcolm loaded the block carefully with every knife he could find.

There was still no sight or sound of Valentine and Malc suspected that the killer was waiting to attack anyone who tried to leave the house. There was a small corner near the front door that was perfect for this purpose, except that it would be cramped and uncomfortable. Malc decided against approaching the probable hiding place and waited in the kitchen instead. He made himself a cup of tea in case he was waiting for a long time.

Valentine emerged 35 minutes later, furious about the delay and aching from the contorted pose he'd adopted in his hiding place. He ran towards the kitchen and raised the weapon he'd used to butcher his victims.

Malc launched nine knives across the room using Sid's malfunctioning Christmas gift and three hit Valentine in the chest. Valentine slowed his sprint to a walk. He looked dumbfounded at Malc who promptly finished his arrest by swinging the heavy wooden block into Valentine's head.

After Valentine's capture, Malc claimed he had deliberately provoked the killer. He said that he'd suspected the killer's pride would demand retribution for Malc's claim of superiority. He also claimed that his argument with Mick was a piece of an elaborate set-up. He graciously identified Mick as a vital co-conspirator in the scheme, an apology for earlier excluding him.

Mick received more credit for his fake contribution to the Valentine case than his real contribution to 23 others. He received the prestige he'd never wanted, but he also received greater respect from his superiors. Their renewed confidence in his hunches will help him add to his many closed cases. This is great news for the city because he is a very talented investigator.

Malc retired from police work. He told everyone that the stress of the attempt on his life had disrupted his thought processes and dented his instincts. His many fans allowed him to retire on a high and wished him well for his new, safer endeavours.

Malc and Mick remain friends to this day. I am told that neither of them speaks to Gary.

By my calculations, I estimate that nine of Gary's fifteen uncles were still speaking to him at this point in the year.

The year wasn't over yet.

Less in touch with reality

I struggled to choose my next step. Part of me was ready to move on, leave the area and start over. Another part of me wanted to see Warwick and hoped to see Caitlyn.

In addition, a stubborn part of me didn't want to admit defeat. I'd already moved from Markden to Larkbridge. Living inside the ring road was supposed to be my compromise, the middle ground between staying and fleeing. I didn't want to be chased away.

In addition to the intermittent physical danger, strangers verbally abused me every time Mal McCall wrote a column. In the first three weeks of June, he offended northerners, the poor, doctors, the old, Muslims, lawyers, armchair sports fans, immigrants, politicians, the French, the unemployed, the Scottish, teachers and the entire hotel industry.

Some extremist Muslims called for Mal's death. So did some extremist teachers.

I was under the impression that things couldn't get stranger. I was mistaken. For several months, I'd upset people I barely knew with columns I wasn't writing. Then in June, people I didn't know at all began greeting me in the street. To maximize how awkward this was, it happened for the first time while I was arguing with Caitlyn.

We met near the tower where she now worked. We ate our lunches quickly and walked the nearby streets with her lunch hour's remaining minutes. The conversation was strained. Our expressions were tense. To the impartial observer, we looked like a couple contemplating a break-up. In truth, we had little left between us to break.

Caitlyn was desperate for a new life free of all the challenges she'd brought with her from her old life. She'd attempted to turn things around with a new job and new friends. She was disappointed with the results.

After a few months as a single woman, she decided to meet someone new. She hoped to find someone with all of my good points and none of the bad. She joined an online dating site, gave them her details and gave them her preferences. The site immediately told her it had a match and the match was me.

The recommendation upset her because she wanted a new beginning and I was central to the life she was trying to forget. The recommendation surprised me because I hadn't joined an online dating agency.

I checked my online profile and I agreed with all the details it quoted. Based on the accuracy of the information, and his track record of providing unwanted assistance, I immediately suspected Warwick. Based on the likelihood of his involvement, as well as her pre-existing willingness to accuse him irrespective of the availability of evidence, Caitlyn blamed my brother too.

Caitlyn had forgiven my earlier connections with a dating agency as an honest error of judgment, but she was angry I'd repeated the same mistake. However, what upset her most was that the online site, with its algorithms and calculations, thought we should try again. She denied this and insisted we argue about my brother instead.

"Why are you defending him? I told you what he said to me."

"He didn't mean harm. He has an unfortunate way of saying things."

My excuse was weak. When my brother says unfortunate things, he often says the unfortunate things to Caitlyn. She knows this, which is unfortunate.

They've never liked each other. The only way I can explain the mistrust and disagreements between two people I love is that Warwick resides in one world, Caitlyn resides in another and neither likes where the other lives.

"Did Warwick tell you to sign up to the dating agency?"

"I told you. I didn't sign up to the site. Warwick must have given them my information."

"But why did he sign you up? Did you ask him to? Did you tell him you'd like to see other women?"

"No."

A woman passed us on the pavement, smiled at me and said hello.

"… Hello." I replied.

"Who was that?"

"I don't know."

"Ray, she spoke to you."

"I don't know her."

"You spoke to her."

"I was being polite."

"If you're seeing someone, you should tell me. You plague me with calls. You beg me to meet you. I don't think it's right for you to see someone else. It makes me feel like a Plan B to your other options. I don't want to feel like a Plan B."

"I'm not seeing anyone. The only person I want to see is you."

She stopped walking and looked at her feet. It's her standard pose for delivering bad news. I've seen it enough times to recognise it.

"That may not be possible. I met someone else on the site. I don't know if it will be anything, but I thought I should tell you. We've known each other for a long time. I want us to be friends."

She looked at me as she finished speaking.

"... I'm confused." I said.

"Why does everything I do confuse you?"

Two women looked at me closely as they passed us. They talked about me without actually talking to me.

"Should I say something?"

"Yes."

"No. I can't. Should I?"

"Yes!"

"No. I can't."

They walked away giggling. Caitlyn looked at me accusingly.

"I don't know them." I said defensively.

"Do you expect me to believe it's a coincidence? You get 78 messages from a dating agency and within weeks half the city's female population say hi to you in the street?"

"I don't know what's happening. I can't explain it."

"I can. You're seeing other women. Why can't you be honest about it?"

"Why are you so jealous if you're seeing someone?"

"That's different. I want us to be friends. I can see other people and be your friend. You want us to get back together. You can't see other people and chase after me at the same time. It's a mixed message."

"You're actually less in touch with reality than ever."

"I see. … I don't think this friendship is going to work. If you can't be honest with me about this, I can't trust you with anything else."

We were about to spit the first line of the argument's next round when a plain, overweight woman approached us nervously. She hovered until we stopped fighting and looked at her.

"I love you." she said.

"You … You what?"

"I've loved you from the first moment I saw you."

"Goodbye Ray." Caitlyn said.

"No, wait."

"I'm sorry." the woman said. "I didn't mean to interrupt. I think it's lovely that you're so close to your sister."

"His sister?"

"This isn't my sister. This is my girlfriend."

"No, she isn't."

"That's right, I'm not … What do you mean I'm not?"

"I've seen his girlfriend."

"You've seen his girlfriend?"

"Yes. He took her to a party. I saw the pictures. She's pretty."

"She's pretty?"

"She's very pretty."

I suspected that the conversation's inefficient structure of the woman's confusing statements and Caitlyn's repetitive requests for clarification might continue for some time. My fear was unfounded and Caitlyn marched away instead. I realised that this development was even less desirable than the inefficient conversation.

"I've caused a problem." the woman said. "I didn't mean to cause a problem. But I had to speak to you. I love you."

"That's very… Who are you?"

"My name is Anna Dash. Seeing you in person made me very happy and I will love you always."

I ignored Anna and ran after Caitlyn. When I caught her, she refused to speak to me. In hindsight, I wish I'd continued my conversation with Anna. She would have answered the riddle that complicated my life for the next month.

A Jack and Jill story

"Any more professions of love?" the barman asked.

"It's 17 since Monday. I'm on track for 30 by the weekend."

The Idiot's barman loved to ask me about my week. I think it helped him feel better about his comparatively uneventful life.

"OK. Explain to me again why you have a sister and your brother doesn't. Go slower this time."

"It's a Jack and Jill story." I said.

I picked up salt and pepper dispensers and a ketchup bottle to represent the different people in my messed-up family tree.

"Jack met Jill. They had a son and they called him Kennedy."

"Kennedy? That's Ned Dwyer, right?"

"Yeah, Ned Dwyer, the one person who liked to hit me before it became fashionable."

I held that thought for a few seconds and then ordered another bottle of beer. When the barman returned, I started to switch the props in and out of the middle group.

"Jill left Jack for Jack. We'll call him Jack 2. They had a son and they called him Warwick. After Jill left Jack 2, Jack 2 met Jill 2. They had a son and they called him Nehemiah."

"Who's Nehemiah?"

"I am. Don't go there. Jack 2 died and Jill 2 married Jack 3, which seems like a big coincidence until you consider how many Jacks there are in the world. They had a daughter and they called her Roberta. And that's why my brother doesn't have a sister. Any questions?"

"I have one. Your name is Nehemiah?"

"I said don't go there."

"Your name is Nehemiah. There's no way I'm not going there."

"I never liked it much. I ask people to call me Ray because it's my real dad's surname. I hated my step-dad so as soon as it was legally possible, I changed my surname back to Ray. I don't like Nehemiah either, but it's the name my dad gave me; I can't bring myself to change it. I just can't bring myself to use it either."

"Your whole life confuses me."

"Me too."

I enjoyed my trips to the bar. Despite all my claims to the contrary, and the lies I told myself daily, the year was taking a toll. I had two remaining safety nets that kept me from falling apart. The first, and most important, was my brother. The second was The Idiot. They were the two places where people still spoke to me.

In July, I lost another safety net.

I sat at the bar with a pint and a plate of food. The barman, with little else to do, asked about the latest professions of love. This seemed to be his favourite topic. I think he found the issue funnier than I did.

He stopped suddenly and the room fell silent. The other drinkers stared at the doorway and then returned their gaze to their drinks in perfect, unrehearsed unison. The same ominous quiet remained. I turned around, almost certain of who I would see.

He's the most ordinary looking man in the world. His appearance suggests he might be someone's dad, which he is. He looks like he might be someone's aging, ill-tempered PE teacher, which he certainly isn't. I'd guess he's in his late fifties, but he could be older. I've never been brave enough to ask.

I remember the first time somebody aimed a gun at my head and told me I was about to die. The seriousness of the situation compelled me to commit its details to memory. The somebody in that story is Ned Dwyer. Before the world hated me, he was there. He paved the trail. He set up the signposts too.

Ned sat on the stool alongside mine. I think he was surprised to see me, but he tried to hide it.

"I'd like a drink." he told the barman. "Charge what you think is appropriate."

Everyone knew that Ned liked vodka. The barman poured a double from their most expensive bottle and charged him nothing.

"It's been a bad day." he explained to no one in particular.

He drank his vodka in one swift motion and replaced the glass on the counter.

"Darren's upset with you. He didn't like what you told him."

"We went to school together." I said, as if this explained anything.

"He mentioned that."

Ned looked around.

"I don't think I've been in here before. I've passed it a few times, never been in. Not sure if I like it."

I looked straight at the barman.

"I am sorry for the disturbance I caused here a few months ago. You should bar me."

The barman's initial, misplaced instinct was to defend me. It was a bad instinct. I'm grateful for it to this day.

"Ray, you don't …"

"You should bar me and you should do it now."

The barman glanced at Ned and then back at me.

"Ray, it's time to leave. You should drink somewhere else from now on."

I nodded and I left. I never drank there again.

Ned was on his way home from a meeting during which his lawyer advised him to report to the police for questioning. It was good advice, but it infuriated Ned who left it to search for someone to punish for his bad news. It was during this search that he found me.

It is difficult to read Ned's mind. However, I would guess the following:

1. I think his appearance at the bar was a coincidence and everything he decided during his visit was spontaneous.

2. My decision to rule out my return to the bar probably saved the bar. Ned has closed places for poorer reasons than the one I inadvertently gave him by drinking there.

3. Later that day, after Ned replayed our brief conversation in his head, he told Darren to blow up my apartment, preferably with me in it.

The deterioration of his entire life

Shortly before the fiery obliteration of almost everything I owned, my popularity with a certain vindictive executive diminished further than the low level I'd already attained. I mention this now so that his involvement in the destruction of my worldly possessions won't surprise you.

Several weeks before my second enforced relocation, Zara Mahon received a small amount of fame, albeit in happier circumstances than my own. Prior to her unhappy marriage, she'd worked as a journalist. It was through this career that she'd met Grant. After she left him, she decided to use her newfound freedom, her spare time and her writing skills in a new career as a blogger. She bankrolled these efforts with her access to comparative riches that I will explain in a moment. Her web articles were equal parts autobiographical reflection, feminist philosophy, charitable initiatives and a metaphorical two-fingered salute to her violent, estranged spouse.

I admit that her eloquent criticism of men is sometimes difficult to read, although it is rarely unfair (and perhaps because it is rarely unfair). However, I was a fan of her work from the moment I discovered it. I wasn't alone. She developed a small, enthusiastic following and her reputation spread quickly with each of her philanthropic gestures.

Grant Mahon was less impressed. His main objections were as follows:

1. Her blog mentioned him a lot. She wasn't nice.

2. Whenever he threatened her site with legal action, she documented his threats in the pages of the site that he'd threatened. She also followed each threat with a detailed and embarrassing account of one of his morally dubious business dealings. She did this repeatedly until he stopped threatening the site.

3. Shortly after my collision with the front of her car, I'd noticed her bags in the back seat. The reason those bags littered the car's back seat was that its boot was full of Grant's most valuable paintings. Zara's blog termed these as a pro-active divorce settlement. In the months following her departure, Zara sold these paintings systematically. Every time she donated a large sum of money to charity, her blog explained which painting's sale had made the donation possible.

I think I might have mentioned that Grant hates to lose. It won't surprise you to know that he hates losing to Zara most of all. Sadly for him, she's tipped the scales so far in her own favour that she'll win every battle he instigates from now until the end of time. Unable to punish her for her crimes, he went in search of an alternate target and selected me. The selection happened like this.

Despite everything she'd suffered, it took Zara a long time to leave her husband. Then, in the minutes immediately after her escape, she second-guessed herself and seriously considered returning. My unexpected appearance in the road tore her from this important decision. In the conversation that followed, I told her that she'd made the right choice. She took this as a sign and resumed her escape, her reinvention and her theft of her husband's art collection.

I know about her uncertainty because she told this story on her blog, with me in the role as anonymous advisor. My anonymity extended to the majority of her reading public. It didn't extend to Grant who'd already identified me as the passenger during that fateful trip.

As such, he acknowledged that I was not his wife's new partner as he had suspected. However, due to my words of encouragement to Zara and the results of that encouragement, Grant decided to blame me for the deterioration of his entire life.

He wanted to retaliate, but the disparity in our previous lives troubled him. It wasn't possible for my life to deteriorate as badly as his life had done because his had fallen from a height that mine had never reached. After much consideration, he decided the only way to punish my involvement to an adequate degree was for him to reduce the quality of my life to the extent that I no longer had one.

This information brings us full circle to the destruction of my apartment.

I didn't see the first explosion, but I heard it. As I turned the corner, I saw the last remnants of the window rain in fragments on the pedestrians below. I watched the cloud of black smoke rise into the sky from a new and gaping hole in the apartment wall. I stood, motionless and dumbfounded, until three smaller explosions snapped me out of my shock.

It said a great deal about my life that I had so many suspects. It could have been Darren. It might have been Gary. I didn't hear the solution to the mystery until Sean Kidder relayed it to me six months later.

In June, the police questioned Ned Dwyer about the information they'd collected from my brother. Ned, on the advice of his lawyer, cooperated in all respects other than providing any information of any value whatsoever.

It was also during June that Darren Rourke had his first argument with King Rat. Darren, minus the entourage with which he usually travelled, attempted to leave the rat's store and found his way blocked.

"What do you expect me to do?"

"It's not my problem." Darren replied.

"I'm making it your problem. You told me to get it. I got it. Now you're saying he doesn't need it."

"Ned's under surveillance. He has to lay low for a few months. Things change. Deal with it."

"If I lose on this, we never do business again."

"Don't threaten me."

"Why?"

"You want me to explain?"

"Yes. That would be really nice." Rat replied calmly.

King Rat knew who he was, what he was and what he did. He was valuable to people, including people more important than Darren, and he knew how much. Darren didn't scare him. The messengers never did.

For his part, Darren remembered that he'd entered the store without his usual backup. He realised that he might have to back down from his tough guy routine or risk upsetting his best supplier.

Darren paused before renegotiating. He hoped the empty seconds would disguise his complete surrender.

"I'll take a quarter of the explosives and a timer. I'll put word about you have more. You won't finish out of pocket."

"If I break even, we stay friends."

Whenever King Rat said friends, he meant person from whom he'd accept money. The next day, word of the available explosives reached Grant Mahon.

At this point, I'm tempted to describe my apartment. Then again, it won't be in the story again because it blew up. In short, it was small, I didn't like it much and the explosion didn't improve it.

Aaron Hayes broke in while I was out. Aaron crept around my home, looking for somewhere to plant the explosive and timer he had in his hands. He heard the door and hid quickly behind a chair.

The door opened and Gary Grey entered. Gary shut the door behind him and looked for somewhere to plant his makeshift bomb.

Aaron waited until Gary's back was facing in the opposite direction and tried to sneak out. Gary turned at the exact wrong moment. They looked at each other's faces and then at each other's hands.

I know how unlikely this sounds, but I promise I'm not making this up. They spoke in person for the first time in the soon-to-be crime-scene of my flat. I'll always wonder what the conversation might have been if they'd spontaneously discussed abandoned cars on steep slopes.

"Are we here for the same reason?" Aaron said.

"It looks like it."

"How about I take this side and you take that side? I'll keep quiet about you if you keep quiet about me."

"It's a deal."

The two men walked to opposite sides of the apartment. Aaron looked around the small kitchen for a suitable location. Gary looked around the small bedroom. Aaron looked behind the washing machine and found a bomb with a timer that read eight minutes. Gary opened the drawer of a bedside cabinet and found a bomb with a timer that read four.

I was on my way home following a night shift. I was later than usual because of the complexity of my final call. You have to complete all your conversations, however long that takes. If I'd arrived one minute earlier, I would have seen Gary and Aaron, empty-handed, sprinting into the distance. If I'd arrived ten minutes earlier, I would have been part of the blast.

The centre of a crisis

The police questioned me for most of the day and treated me as the chief suspect. They wrote up an initial report that alleged I might have a psychological desire to be at the centre of a crisis and concluded I might be responsible. The inspiration for their theories was a phone call from a colleague in Markden.

They released me without charge after seven hours and one of Warwick's minders collected me at the door. I finished the afternoon in Warwick's latest temporary home. I lounged on one of the room's twin beds while my brother slumped in the other. It was difficult to tell from our expressions which of us had narrowly escaped an explosion that would have caused an unwelcome and irreparable distribution of body parts.

"I came here so that you could cheer me up." I said.

"Sorry. I'm not feeling great."

"I lost everything I own. What's your excuse?"

"My brother might go to prison because of me."

"Ned tried to have you killed."

"I know, but he's still my brother. I just need to be depressed about it for a few days."

"You're not thinking of walking?"

"I can't. If I walk, I have to pay for the room service. I don't know how many pizzas that is, but I can't afford it."

He endured many difficult days during the year, but this was the lowest I ever saw him.

"You did the right thing." I said.

"I know and I wish that made me feel better. ... Sorry. I should be saying something brotherly, like ... it'll look better tomorrow."

"You're right. I need to be positive. Do you think there's a beautiful woman out there for me?"

"I don't know. Maybe."

"You said there was a beautiful woman out there for you."

"I'm not sure about that anymore."

"But there are more attractive women than attractive men. What about your spare women theory?"

"I still like the theory and I wish it were true, but the theory's got a serious flaw. I forgot to consider life expectancy."

"Oh, I see where you're going. Women live longer."

"Yeah, there are spare women, but they're all 83."

Warwick's minders hovered behind him, a ritual they performed every time they needed his cooperation.

"You can't stay here tonight." Warwick said. "The police will want you to stay in touch regarding the explosion. They'll need a number and an address. You can't give them me."

The minders faded backwards as soon as he'd delivered the message.

"I understand." I said.

"Do you have somewhere you can go?"

"I don't think so."

"I think I know someone who'll help."

Two hours later, one of Warwick's bodyguards dropped me outside a hotel two blocks south of the city centre. I walked through the automatic doors and met Audrey in the lobby. It said a lot about my situation that my closest ally was a woman whose short-term career prospects revolved around attempts to kill me.

"Explain the deal to me again. I need to understand the arrangement and I need to know how much to blame my brother for it."

"Warwick persuaded me that if I want to observe the events of your life, it would be more convenient for me if those events happened near my hotel."

"And for that you'll pay for my stay here."

"It's worth it. I'm going to save a fortune on gas and cab fares."

"I hadn't realised that the geographical inconsistency of my near death experiences was so inconsiderate."

"I think inconsiderate is too harsh a term. After all, you probably have different priorities than I do."

"I think that's possible, yes."

She showed me to my room and handed me my key.

"I'm next door." she said.

"Anything else I need to know."

"I may have bugged your room."

"You may have?"

"I may have." she confirmed.

'And this was my brother's idea?"

"He's looking out for you."

She was right, but my brother would be the first to admit that when he looks out for me, the results are mixed.

I opened the door. Audrey followed me into the room without invitation.

"Your brother seems a nice guy." she said.

"He is."

"How does a nice guy work for someone like Ned Dwyer?"

"Warwick's dad was in jail and his mother wasn't too interested in being his mother, so Warwick was raised by Ned. Warwick's spent his whole life trying to repay that debt."

"He still loves his older brother."

"Yes, he does."

"But Ned hates you."

"Yes, he does."

"Why couldn't Warwick swing you more protection? Even before Warwick turned, Ned's people targeted you."

"What happened to me is a restrained response from Ned. If it wasn't for my brother, Ned would have killed me long ago."

"What did you do?"

"My dad was in jail and my mother wasn't too interested in being my mother. Warwick looked out for me and Ned looked out for Warwick. When I reached a decent age, Ned offered me work. I politely declined."

"I'm guessing that wasn't well received."

"Ned was being gracious and Ned doesn't do gracious. I doubt it's happened since. He needed to make an example of me or others might follow suit."

"And that's why he hates you?"

"That was his first reason. He's picked up some more since."

"What will you do?"

"I'll watch my back." I replied. "But if I die, tell the police it was probably Darren Rourke."

Every woman over forty hates you

Markden doesn't have any famous people. Ned is important and well known locally, but he would be an anonymous face in almost every other corner of the country. I received more than fifteen minutes of notoriety, but I accidentally borrowed most of that from other people.

Newmill is a different matter. The area that stretches from the southern ring road to the city centre's southern-most streets has produced disgraced politicians, millionaires and award winning actors. Technically, it is also the birthplace of a fictional journalist who until recently was a figment of my imagination.

Another notable Newmill resident is Alistair Radley, the long-since-dead businessman whose statue adorns the pedestrianized centre of Newmill's original high street. His life's achievements are sadly forgotten, but his statue is statistically the most frequently vandalized in England. I suspect that Markden's gangs contribute to that record.

The most famous of Newmill's living sons is a sportsman, Max Cane. He's idolised locally because he plays football for his home city and repeatedly rejects moves to bigger clubs. His achievements include the most number of assists in a single season and the highest conversion rate for penalties in the history of the sport. He also scored a controversial goal for England against Russia in a world cup qualifier that the referee should have pulled back for offside. Soccer fans discuss it in parallel with the '66 World

Cup due to the role-reversal involvement of a Russian team and a German linesman.

Max Cane also has a fanatical following in Thailand due to a successful club tour of Southeast Asia. In a public relations stunt, Max played for the Thai national team against his own club in a demonstration match and scored twice in a 3-1 victory. Every football fan in Thailand has loved him ever since. Even rival fans grudgingly respect him. He's that type of player.

I've never met our worst politicians. All the award-winning actors fled elsewhere a long time ago. The only millionaire I know is Grant Mahon and I'd happily forget those encounters. I've crossed paths with Max Cane though. This is the story of how I met him.

I went to the police station so that they could officially inform me I was no longer a suspect in the demolition of my own apartment. They didn't apologise. They admitted my lack of direct involvement reluctantly, but hinted that I might have deserved it. In addition to their false accusations and ambiguous suspicions, someone from their department sold my departure time to Darren Rourke.

Darren followed me as I left the building. He accelerated when I increased my pace. He chased me when I ran. Five minutes later, as I reached the start of Newmill's high street, he was still with me. I continued to sprint as fast as I could. Despite my efforts, I couldn't shake him.

A crowd blocked the street ahead of me. I glanced left and saw one of Darren's henchmen approach from the left. I glanced right and spotted another two. There was only one route available.

I jumped on the short wall that encircles Alistair Radley's statue. I maintained my high speed and launched myself into the middle of the crowd, hoping its centre would give me the highest concentration of people and the best possible landing. I crashed heavily, the unfortunate and inevitable by-product of expecting people to catch you when you haven't warned them that this might be necessary.

As I picked myself up, I saw camera flashes from some reporters in the crowd. I covered my face and left the area as quickly as I could. Darren couldn't break through the mess I'd created and I escaped.

You may wonder where Max Cane featured in that story. Remember the part where I flew through the air and needed something to break my fall. That was Max. The collision broke his leg and he didn't kick a ball for another nine months.

If you are wondering what I did in a previous life to warrant this streak of bad luck, I don't know what else to tell you.

The next day, I asked Audrey to bring me a newspaper. I didn't want to brave the streets personally until I knew what I was facing. She returned ten minutes later with several back pages. All three ran with the same lead story, fuzzy pictures of the chaotic scene and a glimpse of my fleeing figure. I didn't think anyone would recognize me if these were the best photographs available and I assumed that the papers would have used better pictures if better pictures existed.

"There were 400 people there. I had to collide with the professional footballer." I complained.

"The images are hazy at best." Audrey replied. "I think your identity is safe."

"We have to keep this a secret. If the tabloids get my name, I'll be a target for his team's fans. I'd have to leave the city. I'd probably die if I set foot in Thailand."

"Why Thailand?"

"It's a long story. Do you want to go for a walk?"

"What are you planning?"

"Let's head towards the centre slowly and see if any football fans feel an uncontrollable urge to attack me."

"Sounds like a plan." she said enthusiastically.

Nothing dented my confidence in an idea more than Audrey's approval.

We walked for fifteen minutes. We passed at least 80 people wearing football tops in a show of support for their injured hero. Most of them had Cane's name and number on the back. They didn't look twice at me.

As we neared the edge of the city centre, the demographics changed. We saw less teenagers and more working professionals. The expressions changed and my face appeared to anger more and more people. This was my first clue that I had inadvertently offended another segment of society.

We crossed the street and stalled near the foot of a tower block. Caitlyn's new job was on the building's tenth floor. I looked for her automatically, but all I saw were expressions of disgust of which I seemed to be the cause.

"Audrey, I'm not imagining it, am I?"

"No. Every woman over forty hates you."

Anna Dash, a woman who'd previously professed undying love to me, approached us.

"How could you? I hate you. I hate you."

She slapped my face and walked away in tears.

"You're incredible." Audrey said. "You're the most powerful hate magnet I've ever met."

"Thank you."

"And I've met a lot of really bad people."

"Again, thank you."

"You're welcome."

I'm not sure she always registers my sarcasm.

I'm not proud of the following. I admit it for the sake of the story.

I hid for a week.

Each time I ventured out briefly, I received such a volume of retaliation against crimes I hadn't identified that it became safer to avoid my entire species. I didn't know what I had done. I didn't know how I had done it. All I knew was that my appearance provoked rage in a high percentage of the city's middle-aged, female population.

I picked up my ringing phone reluctantly and hoped it was my brother. He was family. He still liked me. He wasn't female.

"Hello."

"Hi. How are you?" Warwick asked.

"My face hurts, my brain hurts and I'm really, really confused. Please give me some good news."

"I know why you're getting slapped in the street."

I needed to know. I wasn't sure I wanted to.

"OK. I'm listening."

"The show is called Never After. It's a glorified soap, but it's developed a real following. Guess the demographic that loves it. Guess who looks like the main character."

"People think I'm a TV star?"

"His name is Tom Lincoln. He joined the cast two months ago. He's now the show's main bad guy. He split up a happy couple. He stole his aunt's life savings and gambled it away. Oh, and he's slept with three different characters, other than his wife, who he's planning to kill."

"I'm getting attacked because he's trying to kill his wife? What happens if he succeeds?"

My brother laughed unsympathetically. I think he found the issue funnier than I did.

"The actor is dating the actress who plays his wife. She's stunning. Part of me wants to slap you too."

"Thanks brother."

"Don't kill the messenger. I'll keep watching and keep you informed. I'm hooked already."

"Subliminal messages?"

"It's the only explanation."

I added this information to my internal debate about my future.

"Do you want to stay with me for a while?" Warwick asked unexpectedly. "I reckon I can swing it now that you're in the clear for the explosion."

"I didn't think that was allowed."

"I don't think the rule applies to you. It's in place because when someone's around me, it puts him or her in danger.

They're terrified of the bad publicity they'll receive if an innocent bystander is hurt. You're not innocent. You're not a bystander. I can't imagine how you could be in any more danger. All things considered, the rules are a little shakier."

A blackly comic perspective

Caleb Gerrity hates me. His decision to hate me is not unusual, unprecedented or unexpected. Many people hate me. The benchmark for the scale and sincerity with which it is possible to despise me is Gary Grey. It's possible it always will be.

Gerrity is a little different in that, unlike Gary, he has never met me. This is also not unprecedented. Many people who have never met me hate me. The benchmark in this latter group is Tinsulaananda Weerawatnadom, a soccer supporter from Bangkok who has hated the unidentified culprit for Max Cane's injury from the moment it occurred. He's written extensive, online articles on the subject. His irrational and potentially violent attitude towards me is arguably disproportionate to my crime.

Gerrity is a little different again in that his hatred of me is completely rational. He has his reasons for hating me. Compared to other possible reasons to hate me, his are stronger than most.

Caleb Gerrity worked for the division of the witness protection program entrusted with securing witnesses and evidence against Brad Doyle. To phrase it another way, Gerrity was the man responsible for paying my brother's pizza delivery tab.

In the past year, he played a key role in keeping my brother alive. At the same time, my brother risked his life to tip the balance in an on-going case that the police were previously losing. These and other factors may not be foundations for friendship, but they should have produced mutual tolerance. It didn't work out that way.

As I'll explain, a significant part of the problem, like so many problems, was my mother.

She invited me to dinner during another of her melancholy phases that I knew from historical precedent would likely end prior to the actual meal. I didn't know what would replace her melancholic disposition. Candidates included:

1. Anger at everything I've said and done since birth.

2. Resentment of everything I've said and done since birth.

3. Disappointment in everything I've said and done since birth.

I didn't want to attend and I resorted to the most convenient excuse available. I told her I couldn't visit because some people wanted to kill me.

She begged me to change my mind unsuccessfully and then drifted into an unapologetically antagonistic mood, an abrupt and seamless transition whose immediacy surprised even me.

We argued and I ended the call. Over a period of several decades, we've argued a lot and I've ended many, many calls. We've also argued a great deal about the frequency with which I end our calls. It's a regrettable, cyclical pattern that I never resolved because I rejected every solution that removed my option to end calls.

She was furious with me and she was still furious an hour later when Darren knocked on her door and demanded my latest contact information. She gave him my phone number and instructions to educate me on how sons should treat their mothers.

Darren reacts poorly to terms and conditions, but she caught him off guard by providing the number so easily. He phoned me three minutes later and repeated her message in full before reaching the reason for his call. In the tradition of the semi-regular dialogues we'd engineered over the prior months, he provided a description of what would happen to Warwick if my brother testified. It was similar in philosophy to Darren's previous threats.

To his credit, he always varied the details. Also to his credit, the violence he threatened did sound very painful indeed. I would probably have feared for my brother's well-being except for Darren's failure to provide an equally detailed account of how he planned to find us. It was the main weakness to all of his threats.

The following is the basic structure for one of Darren's threats in case you wish to practise at home.

"I will find you (vague or non-existent explanation of how) and then you will regret it (lengthy list of reasons why)."

I didn't object to the threats. From a blackly comic perspective, they were amusing. What annoyed me about this particular call was his delivery of my mother's criticism. If I had wanted to hear her rebuke, I wouldn't have ended the conversation with my mother.

To this day, I can't explain why I disconnected her call and didn't disconnect Darren's. On reflection, hanging up seems an elegantly simple solution. Unfortunately, it isn't the solution I selected. Instead, I said something like:

"Tell Ned that my brother is the least of Doyle's problems."

If I said that I don't know why I said it, it would be a lie. I know why I said it. I was tired and I wanted to retaliate against his delivery of my mother's message. I will confess however that there was a limit to how much I considered the possible repercussions of my statement.

My line of thinking went as far as the following:

1. Darren would interpret what I said as a verbal slip that betrayed a second mole in Brad Doyle's organization.

2. Darren would tell Ned Dwyer and Ned would tell Brad Doyle.

3. Doyle would tear his organization apart looking for a second mole.

Needless to say, this was before I found out that there was a second mole.

My brother had told me his explanation as to why his testimony was so important. He hypothesized that it was a key part of a scheme to get Dwyer to turn on Doyle. We didn't know that Gabriel Velasquez, one of Doyle's former lieutenants and the Spaniard of his organization's United Nations, had already turned.

The wise old crook had agreed to provide evidence against his former boss and all his current colleagues on the condition that nobody knew about it other than his principal contact. Unlike my brother who was in witness protection and moving location twice a month, Velasquez continued to work in the organization that he'd negotiated to betray.

My brother's role in this wasn't what we thought. He was a distraction. He was a focal point for everyone's suspicions. He took Doyle's attention away from other suspects, including those who were closer and far more dangerous.

My brother has made mistakes and his decisions are sometimes flawed. However, in defence of his incorrect assumptions about his value to the police and in defence of my misplaced faith in his assumptions, his hypothesis is slightly more plausible than the actual explanation.

Gerrity's plot to gather evidence against Doyle using Velasquez had made slow, solid progress. Then, I hinted at a second mole to Darren Rourke and everything changed.

Darren called Ned immediately. Ned told Brad Doyle. Doyle tore his organization apart looking for the second mole. He failed to catch the traitor, but the witch-hunt scared Velasquez sufficiently that he severed his cooperation with Gerrity.

Gerrity threatened Velasquez because threats are his default strategy when he's under pressure. His former witness distanced himself further and Gerrity's bosses reprimanded him for his poor handling of the witness.

Gerrity then threatened my brother to come up with incriminating evidence against Velasquez that he could use as a bargaining tool. As a result, my brother guessed the real reason for his invitation into witness protection.

My brother's minders like my brother, their assignment and the daily access to television and fast food that the assignment provides. They reported Gerrity's threats to his bosses. Gerrity's bosses reprimanded him for his mishandling of a second witness and took the case away from him. Gerrity has hated my brother ever since.

Due to the changes in the sting's key personnel, Gerrity's bosses commissioned a detailed review on the operation's progress to date. The final report suggested that Gerrity's investigation, although promising, ultimately did little damage to Doyle's old group. The same report went on to suggest that the only setback to the organization's rise to even greater power was the witch-hunt that I had inadvertently triggered. As such, my verbal slip did more damage to Doyle and his allies than Gerrity's entire operation.

That's how the report ended. It concluded with that precise summation and my name. Gerrity has hated me ever since.

In response to the critical report, Gerrity leaked it to Doyle in the belief that Doyle would target me. It was a petty act that didn't provoke the intended escalation. Gerrity lost his job immediately, whereas I suffered almost no additional consequences. People who'd traditionally seen no reason for my existence continued to see no reason for my existence. Gerrity's attempt to cause trouble didn't influence this viewpoint one way or the other.

However, the leaked report did identify Velasquez, who unbeknownst to Gerrity had contacted Gerrity's bosses with an offer to resume his betrayal with a different handler. Burned by Gerrity, Velasquez withdrew his offer a second time and accompanied it with an immediate relocation to the far side of the globe.

I haven't spoken to Gerrity in a long time. At one point, he got a message to me that detailed all the ways he planned to hurt me. I wasn't worried. He didn't explain how he'd find me.

A paranoid, delusional attention seeker

With Gerrity gone and Velasquez no longer available, my brother became as important to the investigation as we'd mistakenly believed he already was. This gave him more power to dictate the terms of his arrangement. I received permission to stay with my brother indefinitely the minute he requested it.

I stayed. I watched daytime TV. I ate takeout food. My life was event-free for almost three weeks. I had no news of Gary, Aaron, Darren or Grant. Caitlyn was still seeing someone else. Audrey returned to the US to report her interim findings. Mal McCall went on holiday for the summer, although his paper never explained how a fictional person goes on holiday.

We moved to a new location in the afternoon, a rental property forty miles outside of Doyle's territory. After a lengthy, philosophical and largely nonsensical conversation with my brother, I finished my evening by drafting a list of possible destinations around the country. It was time for a new start. All I needed to do was choose where.

However, the following morning I discovered something about my possible destinations that stalled my reinvention. My main reason for moving was to escape my local problems. Unfortunately, I was more unpopular with the rest of the country than I had realised.

I entered the kitchen, scruffy and semi-conscious. Warwick was up before me, showered and dressed smartly. He was at the kitchen table with a coffee and some toast, a restrained breakfast from one of the meal's most fervent supporters. He also looked significantly slimmer than the day before in a sudden transformation that I knew was biologically unlikely. It's possible he held in his stomach for the entire morning.

I should have guessed the reason for all these anomalies, but I didn't.

"Good morning." he said enthusiastically.

I yawned, an approximation of a response and the best I thought I could offer at the time. I approached the table and finally noticed who was opposite him. I woke up immediately.

"Good morning." Audrey said.

She wore a mischievous expression that matched my brother's smile.

"Warwick, is Audrey at the table?"

"Yes."

"She's at the table in your kitchen?"

"Yes."

"She's at the table in the kitchen of your new, secret location?"

"Aren't you pleased to see me?" she asked.

"Don't misunderstand me. To my continual amazement, I like you a lot. However, nobody has tried to kill me in 17 days, 14 hours and about 9 minutes. Your reappearance makes me think that's about to change."

"Nobody knows you're here except for Warwick, some minders, their bosses and now me. But I won't lie to you. You're going to have a bad day. And you might want to sit down."

I lowered myself into a chair slowly.

"While Mal McCall is on holiday, his paper is searching for the most hated person in the country. The results are based on a readership vote of who they don't like."

"Yeah, they're calling it The Loathe List." I said. "I've been reading it this week."

"They've counted down from 100 to 11. Today was the top ten."

I waited for the story's conclusion. Neither Audrey nor Warwick offered it.

"You're not serious. I made top ten?"

"The top seven's the usual suspects." Warwick said. "It's people you'd predict, like murderers, terrorists, government ministers. … But number eight is Mal McCall."

"Mal McCall doesn't exist."

"I guess his column is real enough for him to qualify."

"Half the people who read that column think I write it."

"Yeah." said Audrey. "It gets worse."

"How can it get worse?"

"Number nine is Tom Lincoln."

"I look enough like him to provoke physical violence in complete strangers."

"It gets worse." Warwick said. "Number 10 is …"

"… The unidentified man that broke Max Cane's leg." I guessed.

There were a few seconds of silence as I let the news sink in.

"I'm three of the ten most hated people in the country?"

Initially they didn't respond.

"You're three of the ten most hated, *living* people. I'm pretty sure you wouldn't make top ten if they included dead guys."

"Thanks Audrey."

She looked away, a little embarrassed.

"Sorry. It was the best I could do."

Although they allowed me to stay with Warwick on an unofficial basis, I had to keep clear when the investigators visited. They didn't want me there for the interviews because I offered my brother moral support. It compromised the scenario they'd created that they were his only friends in the world.

I was willing to make myself scarce in return for their provision of free accommodation. The problem was that I was running short of places I could go because, technically, I was in hiding. I was running short of people I could speak to for the same reason. As a result, I started to spend more time with the American who trailed me everywhere whether I wanted her to or not.

We stopped pretending that we were strangers and sat together wherever we went. It seemed silly to do anything else.

"What brought you back?" I asked.

"I'm presenting my findings to the British Government. I have two months to finish the study and write conclusions."

"That's nice. Thanks to Gary's uncles, the police still claim I'm a paranoid, delusional attention seeker, but the Prime Minister wants the details of the attacks on his desk."

"It's not the Prime Minister. I think it's more along the lines of senior aides, but they think you're a really good test case."

"That's great. I'm glad I'm helpful to them."

I produced some mail from my pocket.

"What is that?" Audrey asked.

"I've got a post office box. I pick it up once a week. Why?"

"You know you could get tracked that way."

"Are you worried for my safety or upset that I didn't let you tag along when I checked the box?"

"The second one, maybe. … I was worried for your safety too."

I scanned the contents of the first envelope.

"I've been offered an interview … and it's today."

"What's the job?"

"It doesn't say."

"It sounds like a trap."

"It may be, but my life needs more money and less daytime television. How about I go and you watch from a distance? It would be like old times."

She laughed at my feigned enthusiasm for our old times.

"Let's do it."

The city's gallery ran a survey two years ago to determine why so few visitors pass through its doors on an annual basis. To paraphrase the findings, the most frequent response was surprise that the city has a gallery. They repeated the survey for the residents of other regions to see if visiting tourists were a more realistic target for their marketing initiatives. To paraphrase the findings, the most frequent response was surprise that the city has tourists.

The gallery displays a strange collection of mismatched pieces from different styles and eras. Someone told me that the gallery's aim is to display something to offend everybody. I don't think that's true, but it's fair. I'd visited the gallery twice before, on both occasions with Caitlyn. For my third visit, I walked in with Audrey.

The invitation I'd received was for mid-day and mid-week and the gallery was quiet. I've never seen it crowded. I'd never seen it this empty.

I didn't know what my interviewer looked like. I didn't know if he knew what I looked like. I glided from painting to statue and assessed each new arrival as a candidate for my mysterious, potential employer.

"The older the painting, the more I like it." Audrey whispered. "If someone attacks you in a particularly destructive way, lead them towards the modern art."

"I'll do my best." I replied.

We noticed a man in his early fifties staring at me. Audrey drifted to one side, took out her notebook and pretended to inspect some portraits. As Audrey walked away, the man approached me.

"You're Nehemiah Ray, right? It has to be you. I was told you looked like Tom Lincoln, but it really is remarkable. I'm Ken Keeble."

"It's nice to meet you."

We shook hands. His warm smile and his failure to assault me in the first ten seconds raised the possibility that his reason for the meeting was genuine.

"You said something in the letter about an interview."

"Forget the interview. I want to offer you a job."

I was stunned. I'd decided earlier in the day that my minimum requirement for the meeting's success was the absence of pre-meditated violence. I hadn't allowed myself to think as far ahead as receiving employment. I glanced at Audrey as she returned her notebook to her bag with a disappointed frown.

"The letter mentioned possible work. It didn't say what it was."

"I'm a TV producer and I'm hiring actors for a show. I'm after a certain look and that look is you. I can tell you now, if you want it, the job is yours."

"It's that simple?"

"It's that simple. I'm not at liberty to discuss the details, but you're the only man for the job."

"Are you going to take it?" Warwick asked when I returned to the safe house.

"It would take me out of the city for a few weeks."

"I thought you needed the money."

I did. My finances were a mess and the call centre had fired me due to recent non-attendance. I was reluctant to enter any building my enemies might be watching, including my place of work.

"You should take it. We can catch up in a few weeks."

"Thanks."

We took a few swigs of beer.

"What do you think of Audrey?" he said.

"I sometimes wish she'd help me more and take notes less, but … yeah, she's great. Are you thinking what I think you're thinking?"

I don't know why I asked. I already knew the answer.

"I think she's great too. I was wondering. … Do you think she's too good for me?"

I hesitated for longer than I intended. I love my brother more than I can tell you, but Audrey is a pretty, talented and intelligent woman whom the impartial observer could use as the definition for women who are too good for my brother.

"You do, don't you?" he said.

"No. No. You're a … Any woman would be lucky…"

"Forget it. You couldn't sound any less sincere. Besides, I can't believe I asked for advice from the least eligible man I know."

"What does that mean?"

"Where do I start? You're average looking. You have no friends. You have a sister who hates you. You have a mother that hates you. You have nowhere to live because your home was destroyed for the second time this year. You're broke. Every boss you've ever had has fired you."

"That's not fair." I protested.

"You're right, it isn't fair, but they fired you all the same. Your aim in life is to be a nice person, but you have so many people wanting to hurt you, I guess that's not going so well. You're on the worst run of luck in the history of mankind and you're still moping for a girl who was never as wonderful as you thought she was."

"Don't bring Caitlyn into this."

"You still talk about her like she's something special. I'm sorry. She isn't. She never was."

The earlier comments upset me, but Warwick's remarks about Caitlyn provoked me instantly.

"You're right. I should move on. But I didn't want to hear it from you."

"What does that mean?"

"Where do I start? You're average looking. You only have two friends and they stick around because they want your leftover take-out food. You have an older brother who wants you dead. You have a mother somewhere, we're not sure where exactly. You're broke. You move house every two weeks. You're unemployable because you have no skills whatsoever. Your aim in life is to have no aims in life and that's going really well. You'll soon have the medically recommended weight of someone twice you're height because you have the same daily intake of pizza as the population of Naples. And you're falling for Audrey, the only girl who's noticed your existence in the past eight months. And yeah, she's too good for you."

42% of the country hates me

At the time, I equated my battered psychological state with a physical beating.

On reflection, it is hard to explain why I associated my circumstance so strongly with a beating, given that I am very familiar with what beatings feel like and this, although serious, didn't feel anything like an actual beating.

The cumulative toll finally defeated me. It was the haunting return of everything I had laughed off and refused to deal with. It was every dismissal, every break-up, every lost friendship, every lost opportunity and every family dinner. It was all of this and more, simultaneously demanding my attention.

Everyone has a certain amount of fight in them. I think I previously possessed more than most, but I had none left.

It's not that I wanted my enemies to find me. In truth, I didn't care if they found me or not. The problem was that in taking so few precautions to ensure nobody found me, I guaranteed that somebody would.

The first person to reach me was Audrey.

She looked around at our surroundings, a city centre bar I'd never tried before. She returned her gaze to me and summarised the situation in her own personal style.

"This is the dumbest thing you've ever done."

"Thank you."

"You're better than this. You know what's coming and you're just sitting there like a deer in the headlights. Do you know what that means? Do you have that expression?"

"We have the expression, but we don't have deer. We say cat instead."

"Deer, cat, moose, rat. Whatever you are, you're in the road, you're in the headlights. Get out its way."

"Thanks for the pep talk."

"It isn't safe here."

"Where is? The whole country hates me."

"That's not true."

"No, it's not true. I'm exaggerating. Only 42% of the country hates me."

"42?"

"It's an estimate, accurate to within 3%. I have to allow for the possible overlap of people who despise me for more than one reason."

"Things are going to turn around for you soon. I honestly believe that. But not if you take chances."

"I'm tired of running and I'm tired of hiding. I've tried so hard to be nice and where has it got me? I was mad at Warwick, but he was right."

"He was wrong about a lot too. He feels bad and he wants to apologize."

"Where do you fit into this?"

"He wanted to come after you, but they wouldn't let him leave the safe house. He didn't know who else to call."

Gary Grey walked in and took a seat on the other side of the room. I think Audrey's presence at my table confused him. He was ready to pounce if she left my side for a second.

"I'll distract him." Audrey said as she followed my gaze. "You leave. No harm done."

"You can't interfere. It would invalidate the research."

"Forget about the research. Ray, you have to trust me. You're upset and you're not thinking."

"I am thinking. I'm thinking about last year. Some people take what they have for granted. I never did. I knew how lucky I was. I didn't want more. I didn't ask for more. I wanted three simple things, I had them and I lost them. Grant Mahon just walked in."

Audrey stared directly at me. She looked more serious than I had ever seen her before.

"We can still deal with this." she claimed.

"I didn't mean what I said about my brother. Warwick's a great guy."

"I think so too."

Grant Mahon walked into the men's washroom. I expected him to walk back out two minutes later like he was in a scene from The Godfather.

"My brother's crazy about you." I said.

"I know and I'm flattered. I like your brother a lot more than I probably should, which is an admission you of all people will understand. I truly believe he'll meet someone who's perfect for him when he has the chance to meet more than one woman per year."

"Yes, I think that would improve his chances."

"We still need to get you out of here." she said.

I thought about what she had risked to come here and it helped me regain a small amount of my fight. It wasn't enough for the long term, but it was enough for Audrey to get me out of the room.

"Can we please leave now?" she said.

I nodded.

"But it may be difficult." I added.

"Darren Rourke?"

"He just walked in. He has three friends with him."

"One big, one tall and one ugly?"

"You caught that too?"

"It's hard to miss."

She stood up quickly, drew a gun and circled on the spot in a fluid movement that took my breath away.

"I am an American citizen with diplomatic protection." she shouted. "I can shoot anyone who takes a step towards me and all I'll get is a flight home with a first class upgrade."

Grant Mahon left the washroom as her statement ended. His stare joined those of everyone else in the room. Audrey stared back at each of them in turn and then whispered the next part of her plan.

"This … is when we start running."

She let me reach the door first and we sprinted down the street. Everyone committed to the destruction of my life followed us outside. We took alternate left and right turns for the next ten minutes until we reached an alley I didn't recognise in a rough neighbourhood I avoided.

My body slumped forwards and my arms took some of the weight as I rested on my knees.

"The terms of the assignment said you couldn't get involved."

"This is a good place for the assignment to end." she said. "I don't think you would have escaped this time."

I trusted her judgment and that made the assessment terrifying.

"I'm sorry I dragged you into this." I said.

She didn't reply.

"What happens next?"

"That depends. We haven't lost everyone yet."

"Really?" I said. "Who's still with us?"

Gary Grey leapt from the building behind me. He landed on my shoulders and we tumbled heavily into Audrey. Gary was the first to recover and he rolled on top of me. He pinned my arms to the ground with his knees, grabbed me around the neck and started to squeeze.

Audrey fired into the wall behind us. The shot startled Gary and he climbed off me reluctantly. I dragged myself behind Audrey and rubbed at my aching throat.

"I have family in the police." Gary threatened. "You even think about hurting me, they'll get you."

"My cousin writes speeches for the President." Audrey replied. "I can get your uncles arrested if I don't like how they look at me."

Gary's eyes flicked towards the gun he'd dropped in his fall from the building. Audrey watched him as he debated picking it up again.

"Do you want to be famous?" she said. "I can make it happen. There's a political protest group in London who want to revoke diplomatic immunity because it's misused. I can make you their rallying call."

"You're bluffing." he said, but he didn't move.

"Ray, get out of here." Audrey instructed. "If the others heard the shot, they're on their way. Is there somewhere you can go?"

"There is. Thank you."

Gary watched me disappear into the shadows and it gave him the motivation for the stupid mistake he'd considered for the previous minute. As he reached the weapon, Audrey fired once and the gun bounced away harmlessly.

Gary looked at the blood that painted the floor around him and he collapsed back into a seated position. His face went pale and his voice became the high-pitched whine of a juvenile.

"I'm *bleeding*. My arm is *bleeding*."

Audrey inspected the injured man and calmly explained her decision.

"I didn't think a head shot would hit anything important."

Sorry about the face

Audrey's employers investigated her conduct and concluded that Gary deserved it. The equivalent British agency assumed American bias, ran an enquiry and concluded that Gary deserved it. An outraged political protest group in London who want to revoke diplomatic immunity immediately seized on these findings and threatened to make Gary the test case for a legal challenge. Their enthusiasm for Gary as their rallying call faded after they met him. They issued a statement praising Audrey's restrained response.

However, Audrey's employers also ran an investigation into her public announcement that she could shoot anyone in a crowded bar without any resultant punishment. They considered her statement very embarrassing due to its accuracy. They postponed the remainder of her assignment and recalled her to America.

Warwick's handlers moved him the night of the shooting. I tried to get a message to him and received no response. I heard third-hand that Warwick blamed me for Audrey's recall.

Without Warwick, I had nowhere to live and no reason to stay. I contacted Ken Keeble and accepted his offer. A car picked me up thirty minutes later and took me to the other end of the country. I slept most of the way.

I woke as the car pulled into the parking lot. Ken arrived a second later as my personal welcoming committee.

"Ray, it's great to see you. I'm so happy you came."

"Thanks, but now that I'm here, can you tell me why I'm here?"

He took my bag and walked me swiftly through the fake town that doubled as his show's set. They were so desperate for my involvement that my arrival preceded my start time by twenty minutes.

"We have many talented actors working this show. However, we have two in particular who are extremely popular."

"Tom Lincoln and Tessa Caron."

"That's right. They both have busy schedules and it's sometimes difficult to tie them down to specific filming days. Tom's contract allows him to complete other projects. We support him in that, but sometimes we need him and he's not available. If we can get someone who looks like him, we can show him from the back or from a distance, and then give all the lines to Tessa. If we do it well, no one will know."

I almost laughed at the turn of events.

"... You want me to be Tom Lincoln."

"That's right, but not until we get you in character."

Ken introduced me to three women who collectively looked after each actor's hair, make-up and clothing. They selected some of the clothes they typically held for Tom Lincoln. They styled my neglected hair into something tidier. They shortened my unkempt beard into something more kempt. (It's possible that kempt is not a word. If it isn't, please replace it with an equivalent term that has the benefit of existing.)

As I left the room, Ken Keeble met me in the corridor. I could tell from his smile that he was impressed.

"How do I look?" I said.

"Like the answer to all my problems. I should introduce you to Tessa next. I'm sure she'll think it's a good likeness."

As we returned to Ken's fake town, I saw her for the first time. She looked our way and walked in our direction.

"Stunning, isn't she?" Ken said.

I didn't reply.

For all I know, she had never looked more incredible than how she looked at that moment. She was without doubt the most beautiful woman I'd ever seen and I was speechless.

I admit I've been caught out before. There have been times when I've met a beautiful woman and I've let her appearance distract me. In these moments of temporary stupidity, I've said idiotic things, inane things, things I've regretted instantly. This was different. I literally lost the ability to speak.

I wish I had spoken. She would have realized who I was. I didn't speak. She didn't realize. She punched me in the face.

I spent the rest of the day by the side of the fake town watching the crew set up the lighting. It was probably boring for everyone else. It fascinated me because I'd never seen the filming of a television show before.

I rubbed at my jaw. My face could still feel the effects of Tessa's surprisingly effective right hook. The anger of the swing spoke to an issue I hadn't heard about yet. The technique of the swing suggested a scrappy childhood and perhaps older siblings.

I was still poking my face gingerly when she sat alongside me. I glanced at her and forgave her a second later. I imagine that if you look like Tessa, this happens a lot.

"… I'm sorry about earlier. I thought you were … You know who I thought you were."

"It's a common mistake."

"I'm Tessa."

She offered her hand. I shook it.

"I'm Ray."

"Ray what?"

"Just Ray."

"It's good to meet you Just Ray. And again, I'm sorry about the face."

If this were a movie, there would now be a montage to convey the repetitive experience of the work I completed over the following days. The way they handled Tom Lincoln's absence was with a storyline that involved Tessa searching for her on-screen husband and missing him repeatedly. I think they stole the idea from an old French movie.

I played the part of Tom's hard-to-find character. I was in the distance. I was out of focus. I left the frame a second before Tessa entered it. It was impossible to tell I was an imposter because of the way they filmed it.

Away from the camera, Tessa avoided me.

I saw her glance at me between takes whenever she thought I wasn't looking. Her expressions switched through every available negative emotion. The inconsistent facial clues suggested that she didn't hate me as much as some people did, but that she hadn't ruled that out as a potential way to go.

Two weeks into my contract, Tessa joined me for lunch unexpectedly. I was at The Café, the glorified food truck that parked on the outskirts of the fake town. I sat by myself because I wasn't a member of the permanent cast (all of whom ate together) and I wasn't crew (all of whom ate together). Everyone else grouped together in his or her established cliques.

I smiled a brief hello. She sat down next to me and nibbled at the tiny salad she'd selected for her meal.

"How long are you staying?"

"It's indefinite." I replied. "It's as long as Tom is unavailable."

"Unavailable? Is that what they told you? Tom's dancing a contract-renewal waltz. He's stalling for a raise and he'll wait until the producers cave."

"He's not filming elsewhere?"

"The only thing he's filming is home videos of himself with someone who is not his girlfriend and I can say that for certain because I'm supposed to be his girlfriend and I'm not in it. Don't you read tabloid headlines?"

"I missed that one, but I think I just guessed why you punched me."

"If you're interested, I hear some sites have it available for download."

"Thanks. I think I'll pass."

"Even Tom's screw-ups work in his favour. He'll turn this into a publicity exercise and they'll be even more desperate for his signature. They've called his bluff by bringing you in. I don't know how long they'll get away with it."

"He sounds difficult."

"You have no idea."

"But you dated him."

Tessa smiled, her face turned a shade redder, and then she retaliated.

"You're hoping it was for his looks, aren't you?"

It was my turn to be embarrassed.

"We don't know each other well enough for that conversation."

"I know." I said. "It's just that no one who knows him seems to like him."

"That sounds about right."

"And everyone thinks you're wonderful."

"If you really want to know what I saw in him, it's a tough one to explain. I'll tell you when I've worked it out for myself."

She inspected my face closely.

"You have me very confused." she said. "Someone who looks like you broke my heart."

"I am nothing like Tom Lincoln."

"Keep that. It's your best quality."

We haven't established if I am worth following

For the next two weeks, I rarely left Tessa's company. We shared almost all our scenes and we rehearsed together when they didn't need us on camera. She was fanatical about learning her lines and recruited me to play the parts of whichever colleagues couldn't join her for an additional read-through. Within days, she'd taken to linking her arm in mine when we travelled between scenes.

She didn't mean anything by this. She's a flirtatious person by nature and I'd noticed her link arms with the other cast members. Yes, we became good friends, but good friends only. I was never confused. I knew exactly what our friendship was and wasn't. However, I can understand how someone might have thought there was more to it.

Walter was confused. Walter was confused enough for both of us. He was probably there before I saw him, but I didn't see him until Tessa told me to.

It was because of Tessa that I didn't notice him earlier. I enjoyed her company. She distracted me from my problems. She made me forget what had happened that year. I lost my instinct for suspicious activities. I lost my radar for the unwanted attention of strangers.

Tessa and I walked from The Café towards the evening shoot. We were arm in arm, as we often were. Tessa suddenly seemed distracted.

"I think we're being followed."

"I'm so sorry." I said. "There are people … I honestly didn't think …"

She smiled, mostly at my expense, and brought my sentence to a halt.

"Don't take this the wrong way. I'm sure you're a popular guy, but I think this is a Walter."

"A what?"

"He's a Walter, a stalker. Tom has three. I forget the details. One of them is called Walter, so that's what I call all of them. Tom's got restraining orders, but you're not Tom, so I don't know how that works."

"I've inherited three stalkers?"

"Congratulations. They're an actor's ultimate status symbol."

She waved a subtle signal to a security guard who immediately looked in Walter's direction. Walter disappeared behind cover.

"You'd think his stalkers would be women." I said.

"I don't know the deal with all of them. One of the Walters is in love with me and thinks he has a chance if he gets rid of Tom."

"Any chance they might attack me?"

"I don't know. I mean, they haven't yet."

This didn't make me feel a whole lot safer.

Over the next few weeks, I paid more attention to the people who hung around the set and who never appeared to work. They may have been fans. They may have been stalkers. They may have been staff who received a good wage for doing very little. It was difficult to tell the difference.

The Walter called Walter was there the most. I knew that security had waged a war to keep him away and lost. I knew he ignored court orders. Most of all, I knew I would go insane if he continued to hover on the periphery of my life.

I needed some resolution. I thought through all the options available to me and I didn't like any of them. Eventually I resorted to the only plan I hadn't eliminated. I spoke with him.

I tracked him down to one of the alleys behind the fake town's main street. It was an ideal location for watching the rehearsals or dodging the security guards. I sat down alongside him. He avoided eye contact for an incredibly awkward minute, but turned to face me when he realised I wasn't leaving.

I selected a technically accurate and non-confrontational opening line.

"I understand you take an interest in Tom Lincoln."

He hesitated and then nodded.

"Are you aware that I am ... *not* Tom Lincoln?"

He nodded again. I suspect I had his attention because I hadn't attempted to remove him forcefully from an area he was legally forbidden from entering. I took this as permission to keep talking.

"OK. Good. That's one of my questions answered. ... I've noticed that recently you have taken an interest in me. I'm a little confused by that because I can think of many reasons not to. And even if I ignore the sociological implications of your actions and the psychological disadvantages to everyone involved, I still don't see what is in this for you."

He looked confused by my concern for his well-being.

"You want to follow him. OK, but he's not here and as you've already confirmed, I'm not him. I suppose you could follow me because you want to follow someone who isn't available and I look like him, but I don't see how your usual motives would apply."

"You've lost me."

He should adopt these words as his life motto. These three words ably describe Walter's entire repertoire of facial expressions.

"I'm asking, politely, from your point of view, why are you stalking me?"

"Oh, I see." he said. "That's a good question."

He gave it some serious thought.

"First of all, I should mention, just a preference, but I don't like to call it stalking." he said.

"What do you call it?"

"I like to think of it as in-depth research."

"Between us, it must take a lot of effort."

"Oh, it does. It really does."

"It seems like not the best use of your time to put so much effort into following me when we haven't established if I am worth following."

"Yeah, I can see that argument."

"Think what you could do with all that extra time and energy."

"It's true." he admitted. "I sometimes don't have much spare time."

I grinned, as if we'd reached mutual agreement on a joint solution.

"Then we're agreed. You'll stop following me. You'll try something else with your time. We'll see how it goes on a trial basis."

"I'm not sure about this." he mumbled.

"It's not forever. It's just until we determine whether I am worth following."

"... OK ... That seems reasonable."

"Excellent. I'm glad we talked."

I walked away smiling. Walter walked away confused.

I hoped I'd made a strong case. I must have been moderately successful because I didn't see him for the next two weeks.

As pathetic as I am

I've never experienced love at first sight. I now consider that time wasted. I love Caitlyn and it's a mystery why I took so long to make up my mind.

However, I have seen love at first sight. That split second when Warwick first saw Audrey, it was obvious to everyone in that room. It's true that one of his bodyguards later claimed that my brother should have spontaneously experienced 'She's too good for me at first sight' instead, but I won't criticise my brother for his instinct. I stubbornly adored someone whose strategic foundation for an entire year was my absence.

Sean Kidder confessed to me that he's experienced love at first sight too. He enjoys travelling, he is a huge fan of The Beatles and John Lennon, but I don't think there is anything in his life that compares to his love for Tessa Caron. He is, somewhat against character, a huge fan of her show. The worst day of his year was the episode in which her character died, a shock twist that split audience opinion when it aired in late December.

"I don't believe you can fall in love at first sight with just anybody." Sean told me once. "I do believe you can fall in love at first sight with Tessa Caron."

He really likes her. And please don't underestimate the implications of the really in that sentence. It's intended to carry significant implications, much like when I tell you that Gary is really thin, it can really rain in Markden or I really don't like it when people shoot at me.

He admitted reluctantly that the Christmas Day episode was great. It was. He said that they'd regret writing her out of the show. They did. He said the show wouldn't be the same. It wasn't.

However, despite the above, I sympathise with Ken Keeble and his team of writers. They wanted to please their core audience, the viewers who liked Tessa but who loved hating Tom. Tessa and Tom couldn't work together. As soon as he returned, she had to leave.

Shortly before Tom's return, I spent most of my free time with Tessa. It was an easy, mutually beneficial friendship. We would hang around on the set after each scene finished. It was a habit that the crew frowned on because they didn't want the cast to get in their way. We were the exceptions because they adored Tessa (for being Tessa) and tolerated me (for not being Tom).

Tessa and I talked endlessly. She told me her real name was Esther Carson, named for a great aunt. She'd changed it to distinguish herself from a television veteran with a similar name. I admitted my real name was Nehemiah. She encouraged me to become an actor so that I could change it.

I can't remember all the conversations with Tessa, although I do remember enjoying every one of them. We bonded over a shared appreciation for Zara Mahon's blog and Tessa's intention to donate money to one of Zara's causes. We agreed that her television show might be implausible nonsense. Tessa admitted that she'd like to be in a James Bond movie. I suggested that if given the opportunity to appear with 007, it might be more fun to attempt world domination than to prevent it.

The conversation I remember the most is when she asked about Caitlyn.

"Do you have a girlfriend?" she asked in a sudden departure from every previous part of our conversation.

"Do we know each other well enough to have this conversation?"

"You know all about me. I'm playing catch-up. Do you have a girlfriend?"

"... No."

"I don't understand that because everyone I know likes you."

"It's been a difficult year."

"Let me guess. You were deserted by a long-term girlfriend of … three years?"

"Four years. She said she needed to clear her head."

"Have you given up on her?"

"I don't know. I didn't want to, but maybe it wasn't to be."

"What does that even mean?"

"Every time I arranged to meet her, something went wrong. A Tom Lincoln fan interrupted us and told me she loved me. I was arrested for something I didn't do. I got hit by a car."

"You got hit by a car?"

"It was a nice car."

"I'm glad. If you're going to be hit by a car, it might as well be a nice one."

"One of these days, I'll tell you who was driving it and you'll be even more impressed... Anyway, it was the most amazing streak of bad luck and every time I tried to explain, my excuses sounded far-fetched. Caitlyn didn't believe me. I barely believed me. She stopped returning my calls and the last I heard she was seeing someone else."

"She made a mistake. You're the nicest guy I've ever met."

"Tom's an idiot. You're the most amazing woman I've ever met."

She leaned across and kissed me on the check. Then she took my arm and rested her head on my shoulder.

"Why am I still in love with the unreliable, lying cheat?"

"Tell me if you work it out. Maybe it's the same dumb reason I'm in love with someone who left me nine months ago."

She sighed, full of regret, but momentarily content.

"Thank you for being as pathetic as I am."

"You're welcome."

As an aside, if you are suspicious of any part of the last few pages, you'll join good company. I've survived more than 100 attempts on my life. I've talked to the CIA about self-preservation techniques. I was arguably the turning point of a football season followed worldwide by millions. However, if Tessa becomes as famous and as popular as I think she will, Tessa kissing my cheek will one day be the turn in my tale that people won't believe.

Whether or not you believe the above account, there was at least one person who'd noticed how close Tessa and I had become. Two weeks after our mutual decision to divert his attention elsewhere, Walter resumed his daily pilgrimage to the studio. I saw him late morning and tracked him down to a different alley that carried the same advantages as his previous haunt.

"I thought we agreed you wouldn't follow me."

"We did." Walter conceded. "And I did, I stopped following you. Then I couldn't find him, I followed her, and she was with you."

"So, you're following her again?"

"No, I'm following you."

I hesitated until I regained my composure.

"OK. ... *Why?*"

"I saw her with you and she obviously likes you."

"She likes me as a friend."

"You're saying she doesn't love you?"

"She still loves him."

"She isn't with him. She's with you."

"That's because she doesn't like him."

He looked confused again. His confused expression is genuinely world class.

"You've lost me."

"OK. Let's go back a step. You follow the man she's with because you want her to be with you. "

"Right."

"But, she'll never be with me, not in the way you think, because she doesn't love me. She loves him, but she'll never be with him again because she doesn't like him. So, there's no one left to follow."

"And she'll never be with me?"

"No, she'll never be with you."

"Is that because she doesn't think of me that way?"

"No, it's because you're a dedicated researcher and you're too dedicated."

He stared at his feet for ten seconds that felt longer while he considered the latest information.

"So, you're saying I should stop following you."

"Me, him, her, yes."

"And, are you saying, I actually improve my chances with her if I stop following you."

"Walter, I won't lie to you. Your improved chances are not the central piece of the point I was trying to make. That said, it would potentially prompt a very marginal improvement to a microscopic possibility."

"Ah ... Hmm ... I'll need to think about this."

"I understand."

"It's a lot to take in."

"Take your time."

He did. It was painful to watch.

"You know, thank you. You've been very decent about all this."

"It was no trouble." I said.

"Not everyone is."

"I can imagine."

After that conversation, I never saw him again. I actually miss him. I can't give a single, sensible reason why.

Not famous enough to be attacked

Ken asked to see me at the end of the day and I found him in his makeshift office.

"Is there a problem?"

"No. I wish you could solve all of my problems as perfectly as you solved this one. I do have some news though. Tom Lincoln signed a new contract this morning. He'll be back at work tomorrow. I'm sorry it's short notice."

"We knew it might happen."

"I thought you might like to say good-bye to people. You're very popular for a guy who's only been here eight weeks."

"Thanks. I'll do that."

For the rest of the conversation, Ken Keeble was complimentary and grateful. He seemed determined to part on the best possible terms. I think he was preparing for Tom's next contract dispute.

I looked for Tessa first and I found her hiding near the set.

"Have you heard about His Highness?" she said. "Look at everyone's faces. It's as if a dark cloud descended. … I love these people and I get so angry at the way Tom treats them. Promise me you'll turn up every time Tom lets them down."

"I'd like that."

"I've actually enjoyed coming to work while you were here. I'm thankful for that."

"I'll always be glad I met you."

"I'll always be glad I met you too."

She gazed across at the set and all the preparation for that day's scenes.

"It will feel so strange to not be here."

"Not here?" I said. "Where will you be?"

"Haven't you heard?" she said. "It's the big, Christmas Day story. Tom kills me."

I'd wondered what would happen to a poor Tom Lincoln look-a-like if Tessa's character died. I was about to find out. I decided that the first thing I would do after my return to my hotel room was shave. It was time to look less like my least favourite actor.

After my farewells, I spotted twenty photographers crowded behind the barrier on the edge of the town. I'd never seen them before.

"They heard Tom was back." a security guard explained. "They swarmed within an hour."

One of the photographers lingered in the shadows of the trees that lined the road. I don't know why I inspected him more than the others. The closest thing I have to an explanation is that he looked evil. I asked the guard about him.

"His name's Zack Regan." the guard replied. "He's a freelance reporter and photographer."

I'd heard about Regan. Tessa estimated that half of the fiction that the papers repeatedly quoted about her had started as a lie in a Zack Regan exclusive.

"He's one of the nastier ones." the guard added.

"Nasty how?"

"Most of the reporters are decent guys. They make a fuss, but they make a living. He's different. He picks fights to get pictures of stars losing their temper. He causes crashes when they try to drive away. He's a problem, but you should be OK when he realizes you're not Tom."

"I'm not famous enough to be attacked?"

"That's it exactly. Be glad of it."

As I tried to make my way to the waiting taxi, they bombarded me with questions about Tessa, Tom and home videos. Each of them stepped back when they realized who I wasn't.

"I know. I'm sorry. I'm not him." I confirmed.

Only Regan pursued me as far as the taxi.

"You're the one that played Tom while they scrapped over contracts."

"No comment."

I opened the door. Regan closed it again.

"I heard Tessa has a new man. Do you know who?"

"No comment."

"That means you know. Is it someone new? Is she back with Tom?"

"No comment."

I opened the door again.

"Tell Tessa we'll find out. Tell her *I'll* find out."

I stopped responding. He wasn't listening anyway. I climbed in and told the driver my destination.

"He reminds me of someone." Regan said.

He said it to himself, but one of the other reporters replied.

"Really? I wonder why?"

"That's not it."

"It's not a conspiracy Zack. You took his picture. You take lots of pictures"

"That's not it. I never forget anyone I've photographed. He's someone I didn't get."

His eyes widened as the taxi pulled away. He remembered where he'd seen me.

After months of media speculation and internet conspiracy theories, Zack Regan identified me as the man who'd collided with Max Cane. He announced it through a tabloid back page with a headline of Villain. He accompanied it with a photograph of me that my mother gave him.

People who don't like me

You may be wondering why it is that my mother gives my photograph to everyone who asks for it. The reason is that she tells our story to anybody who'll listen and she complies with the requests of anyone who takes her side. The people who ask her about me are never on my side.

In this case, Regan didn't like the first picture she offered him. He asked for one in which I looked more suspicious and she happily found him an alternate.

After the story broke, I was instantly unpopular with several million more of my fellow citizens. I'd already considered relocating to a different city, but this latest development prompted me to consider further afield. I drafted a list of possible countries and, for reasons you might recall, Thailand didn't make the cut.

I was at my hotel when I heard about the exclusive. Although my contract was over, the TV company had paid in advance for the room and I had two days left. I decided to give myself those two days to select from the available destinations.

I stalled indecisively on the decision and delayed my tactical retreat. On December 1st, forty minutes before my checkout time, I was no closer to deciding my next steps. I had options. I couldn't persuade myself on any of them.

My rescue arrived from an unexpected source. I glanced through the keyhole cautiously in response to a polite knock and opened the door to one of the few people I considered a good friend.

"You better come in." I said.

"I guessed you had secrets." Tessa replied. "I did *not* guess this."

She had a newspaper in her hand and I could make out the giant V of the Villain headline on its back page. I could tell from her expression that she found the issue funnier than I did. She sat down in the far corner, near to a window I'd avoided for the past two days.

"What's next for you?"

"I have no idea." I replied.

"So, what happens when you leave here today?"

"I have no idea."

She smiled. She had a suggestion and she liked it more with each passing second.

"You told me once that you worked on a complaint line."

"It's as much fun as it sounds."

"But you can take abuse?"

"I am world-class at taking abuse."

"I have somewhere you can stay, for free, for a month."

"That would sound perfect if it didn't immediately follow a question about taking abuse."

She invited me to sit down and I took the far edge of the bed.

"I have an elderly relative." Tessa said. "She lives alone in the middle of nowhere. She can look after herself, so I don't need a housekeeper. But, what if she fell? What if she injured herself? I don't want to think about it. I need a human panic button. I need someone in the house to do absolutely nothing unless he or she hears screams of agony and terror."

I hesitated. It was a kind offer, but it was very different to the possibilities I'd considered for two days.

"She probably won't need you." Tessa added. "She probably won't want you. It's for me. I need someone in that house to make *me* feel better."

She sensed my inner-debate and offered an additional incentive.

"She doesn't have a television and she doesn't follow sport."

"When do I start?"

Tessa's great aunt, the Esther Carson after whom Tessa was named, was a wealthy, independent woman who lived in grounds three miles from the nearest village. She was elderly, but Tessa's increased concern was due to a recent car accident. Esther had walked away with cuts, bruises and a concussion when it could have been much worse. It was bad enough. The doctors said the shock of the impact was the equivalent of adding fifteen years to Esther's age.

We completed most of the journey in silence. Everything Tessa wanted to ask was something I didn't want to discuss. I eventually opened the conversation with a topic in which I wasn't a component.

"What caused the crash?" I said.

"She was caught speeding and she tried to outrun the police car." Tessa answered.

"Somehow, that isn't the answer I expected."

"She has speeding tickets from six different decades. She's very proud of that fact. When I was young, my father banned me from riding in any car she was driving."

Esther is not an average pensioner. This short story was the closest I got to understanding that before our arrival at Esther's home.

"I should warn you." I said. "That article isn't the whole story. There are people who don't like me as much as you do."

"I should warn you." Tessa replied. "Esther doesn't like anyone."

Esther's house was a beautiful two-storey cottage. It looked like something out of a Jane Austen novel. Actually, I can't prove that because I haven't read any Jane Austen, but it did look like something out of a trailer I saw once for an award-winning BBC adaptation of a Jane Austen novel.

We parked in the small courtyard outside the main door and Esther met us at the entrance. She looked at me and sighed.

"Oh. You brought me another one."

I don't know a word that adequately conveys the lack of excitement she communicated with her opening line.

Tessa followed Esther into the cottage and motioned for me to follow. Once inside, they argued for ten minutes as if I wasn't there. They detailed names, events and family history I didn't know as evidence of the other's flaws. Neither looked surprised by the other's accusations and I suspected they'd enacted this exact conversation before.

Esther looked like the Joan Hickson Miss Marple. She talked like the Judi Dench Lady Bracknell. It was a distinctive contrast. She looked like she might collapse any second. She would probably outlive us both.

She turned to me without warning and dragged me into their debate.

"You think I'm lucky, don't you? You think I'm lucky to have a niece who looks out for me like Tessa does."

"I don't believe in luck." I said.

"Neither do I."

This was the first time we agreed on something. It didn't happen again for some time.

"Zoe 3, the last girl Tessa brought in to look after me was the sweetest young thing. I made her cry after one day. She quit after three. You look like sterner stuff. It may take a week to get rid of you."

"Aunt Esther, we've only just arrived and you've already planned his departure?"

"Tessa, my dear, I planned his departure *before* you arrived."

Esther turned to face me again.

"Do you want me to list the irritants she's sent my way? The first was Conrad 4, the least amusing man on the planet. He said I didn't smile enough. He made it his mission to make me laugh. He was blissfully oblivious to his personality's failings until I explained them to him. Laura 6 wanted to check I was OK every seven minutes. I invented long, complicated tasks for her, just so she'd leave the room. Ron 1 ignored me and talked to Tessa instead. She fired him before I had a chance to and I wanted a chance to."

"What's the number after each name?" I asked.

"That's the number of days they lasted and don't interrupt. Justin 5 insisted on lecturing me about appropriate behaviour for someone of my age. He was as stubborn as he was condescending. My usual methods didn't work. I had to throw plants at him."

I looked around for possible projectiles. Esther followed my stare and guessed the reason.

"You're safe. I threw most of them at Justin 5 and Tessa confiscated the rest. Now, who was next?"

"Erica." Tessa prompted.

"Oh yes, Erica 4. I caught her in my jewellery box. I caught Greta 5 in the liquor cabinet. I caught Mina 6 on the phone discussing how terrible I was. She was right. I am terrible. I fired her anyway."

"It's an impressive record." I said.

"That brings us to the aforementioned Zoe 3 who left because I called her mean names. She wanted to help me. She saw my frail, feeble body and she was desperate to help. She couldn't stop herself. I stopped her. Then I made her cry. Then I made her quit. Now I have you. …. Why are you smiling?"

"You told me your secret."

"And what's that?"

"The secret is to do nothing for you."

"You'd let a feeble, old woman like me do everything for myself?"

"When you want help, I'm yours. Until then, you're on your own."

"Oh, you're going to be a challenge. I like challenges."

"I may even last the week." I said.

She didn't appreciate my confidence.

"Don't get ahead of yourself." she whispered.

Tessa gave me her mobile number and promised to pick me up if Esther fired me. She half-expected to collect me that evening.

After Tessa left, the abuse started immediately. Esther's criticisms were insightful and frequent. Her insults were creative and brutal. They didn't upset me. I'd heard worse.

I weathered her attacks for several hours before she summed up our arrangement.

"I hope you're embarrassed by how much of a mess your life is."

"Who says my life is a mess?"

"You're here with me by choice." she said. "Trust me. Your life is a mess."

I avoided her for the rest of the evening. It seemed my best shot at keeping my job.

Esther's health was poor. Her quality of life was a fraction of what she'd enjoyed two months earlier. What bothered her most was the loss of her independence. She needed me. She hated needing me.

With this in mind, I set in motion my strategy for living with Esther. My approach was simple. I made sure that my response to everything she said created a task for her.

She told me she needed something from a top shelf. I brought her a stepladder. She complained about a local politician. I brought her a pen, paper and his mailing address. I hoped that the less I did for her, the less she would resent my presence. I knew I was on the right lines when she asked for my opinion on the curses she'd used in her letter to the MP.

It was gradual at first. The insults per day dropped from 90 to 30. The frequency of the deliberate provocations diminished with each one that failed. The threats of violence never materialized, although I was grateful she'd lost access to houseplants. She referenced repeatedly that she was bad company and knew it. I didn't agree, but I didn't correct her. I continued to do everything she specifically requested and almost nothing she didn't.

After the week of abuse she'd predicted I wouldn't outlast, she switched her approach from criticism of me to criticism of Tessa. Listening to her slander Tessa was difficult, but I didn't retaliate.

"You think I'm unkind to my niece, don't you?" she said after she'd delivered a longer rant than usual.

"I didn't say that."

"I didn't say you said it. I said you thought it."

"I'll keep my thoughts to myself." I replied.

"Fine, but if you don't speak up, I will. Tessa works in a career I don't respect and in a show I don't watch. She dates men I don't trust, hires people I don't like and gives me help I don't want. Tell me one thing she's done of which I would approve."

My instinct was to remind her of how much Tessa loved her, but something told me that this was what she expected. I went with my second answer.

"The first time we met, Tessa punched me in the face."

Esther almost smiled.

"It really hurt." I added.

"Did you deserve it?" she asked.

"Not even a little."

She contemplated the story and I knew I'd scored a point on Tessa's behalf. I used the quiet and the temporary goodwill as an opportunity to push my point further.

"I think you and Tessa have a lot in common." I said. "I wish that would bring you together instead of causing friction."

"She wishes that too, but I can't say I share her enthusiasm." Esther replied and I knew the moment had passed. "Maybe we would get along better if she didn't insist on treating me like I'm a good person at heart. I'm not good. I'm old. Those two characteristics are completely independent of each other. I was consistently and reliably unpleasant for most of my life. To pretend I'm a good person now is disingenuous to all of my efforts. As for my being old? That is simply a matter of not dying. I refuse to accept recognition for not dying."

I didn't reply, but due to personal experiences, I considered not dying a commendable feat on many important levels.

An approximation to a friendship

After another week, she switched her attention to complaining about people I didn't know. Listening to her slander strangers was easier than hearing her slander Tessa. I listened politely. In return for my attentiveness, she didn't immediately end my employment. It wasn't pretty, but it worked. Eventually, we engineered an approximation to a friendship. I've made enemies everywhere I go. Maybe this trait helped me to make a connection with someone who never makes friends.

"Why are you doing this?" she asked. "Are you trying to impress my niece?"

"It's not like that. I needed somewhere to stay."

"So, I'm a hotel?"

"Yes, a hotel, a cheap one."

"You make a girl feel so special."

"Well, it had to be something. It's not like you're good company."

She smiled. She denies to this day that she smiled. She claims to this day that she has never smiled.

"Do you know how old I am?" she said.

"I have the strangest feeling you're 83."

"That's right. How did you know?"

"My brother predicted it. ... It's a long story."

"He must be a clever man." she said.

"Not even a little bit." I replied.

She asked about my motives again the following day. Either she'd started to like me or she needed ammunition. I chose to believe the former and prepared myself mentally for the latter.

I told her about my troubled relationship with my mother and sister. I told her about my brother's legal troubles. I told her about Caitlyn. I skipped over the attempts on my life. She listened quietly to my story and paused after I had finished.

"I want you to know something." she said finally. "When I said your life was a mess, I said it to be mean. If I'd known how messy your life truly was ..."

"You would have said it earlier?"

She shrugged. She would have said it earlier.

On Christmas Day, I cooked a meal for her and we ate together. It was the first time she'd permitted someone to do either of these since her accident. We talked non-stop and solved the world's problems between us. It was one of the best days of my year.

There are amazing women in this world. Some of them are 83.

Tessa visited on Boxing Day. I wanted it to be a peaceful reunion between two women I hoped could be friends again. The peace lasted for twenty minutes and then Esther rebuked Tessa for hiding me instead of helping me.

I pretended I hadn't heard the onslaught and hid in the library. I pretended to be half way through a book I'd picked up twenty seconds earlier. After Tessa found me, she didn't speak for the first minute. She paced the room wearing an expression of shock.

"... I think she *likes* you."

"I know. I'm suspecting that too."

"I mean, in her own way."

"Yes, that's true. It would have to be her own way."

She sat down next to me.

"I'm supposed to solve your life for you."

"I appreciate her request, but I'm the first to admit that my life defies an obvious method of repair."

Tessa thought through everything Esther had told her.

"She's right."

"About what?"

"I gave you somewhere to go. That was the right thing to do at the time, but I'm not a good friend if all I help you to do is hide."

"I like hiding. I've greatly enjoyed hiding. I think I have a lot of untapped, previously unidentified skills as a hider."

"Your life defies an obvious method of repair. Let's aim lower. Let's fix one thing."

She stared directly at me in a way that demanded my attention. I imagine when you look like Tessa, this technique works on the vast majority of attempts.

"Sometimes we can't have what we want and it doesn't matter how much we want it." I said seriously.

"Let me worry about that. If you had one wish, what would you wish for?"

"I don't know anymore."

"Yes, you do." she said.

We both knew she meant Caitlyn.

"I have a confession to make. She's too good for me in almost every way. I've known this for a long time. It's possible she's worked it out too."

"What is the most amazing thing in the world?" Tessa replied.

"I don't know." I answered lazily.

"I know a lot of great guys. If I asked them to tell me the most amazing thing in the world, most of them would tell me that they are. If I asked you, you'd tell me it's Caitlyn. You think she could do better? What's better than someone who cares about you as much as you care about her?"

"I don't know." I answered honestly.

My recent, three-word answers were the same. My tone was completely different.

"When was the last time you spoke to her?"

"It's been a long time."

With a little more thought, I could have provided the exact number of days, but my ability to do this somehow seemed less impressive than it once had.

"I know you want me to drop this. Maybe I should. Let's make one phone call and find out if she's seeing anybody. If she is, I promise I'll change the subject."

"After everything that's happened, I wouldn't know what to say to her."

She handed me her mobile.

"OK. Who else would know?"

I dialled a number from memory for the witness protection program and spoke to one of their officers. He took a message and my number. Warwick called me ten minutes later and I learned three things.

1. He forgave me for Audrey's return to America and he missed me.

2. Ned had a cut a deal, immunity for testimony. We were back on Doyle's radar in a very bad way.

3. Caitlyn was single again and she was trying to find me.

I could have used his news about Doyle as an excuse to keep clear. I didn't. Despite the risks, I decided to see Caitlyn. I didn't want to speak to her by phone. I didn't want to write her a message. I wanted to see her. I asked Tessa for help and she gleefully booked a hotel and a hire car through the studio's travel agents.

I arrived on New Year's Eve.

My unpopularity is rarely helpful

The Drifter is one the tale's most interesting characters and the one I know the least about. I'll tell you the legend because it's the only part of his story I know. I apologize for any widely held inaccuracies I repeat.

The Drifter is a killer. He's a murderer for hire and he's very talented at what he does. He travels through Europe and North America, changing his appearance, his accent and his back-story as he goes. He stays in each city for several months and collects money in advance for four separate hits. At the end of his stay, he kills four people and moves to another city.

He's credited with some high profile assassinations. He's blamed for some things he didn't do. He's shown no interest in distinguishing the truth from the fiction because all of it contributes to his infamy. The rumour and anonymity combine well for both him and his legend.

His only colleague is an associate who advertises The Drifter's availability for work. Even less is known about her. All I can say is that in early December, a woman appeared in the city that was home to some of my worst enemies and enquired about potential customers. She spoke with several local criminals, including King Rat.

For his part, King Rat contacted a handful of people who he thought might be interested in hiring The Drifter. Given King Rat's involvement, it was only a matter of time before someone offered my name.

Gary still obsessed over my perceived influence on my sister. Aaron still had nightmares about my supposed attempt on his life. Darren was scared that Ned Dwyer's testimony might be blamed on his failure to intimidate me. Then my face appeared on a tabloid's back page under a headline of Villain and they all remembered their unfinished business. It was as they contemplated this that someone offered my death for a price. I'm not surprised they considered it.

My unpopularity is rarely helpful. There were few moments it was less helpful than this.

The Drifter's associate set up a stall in the snow on a busy pedestrianized street, a couple of roads from the apartment my enemies blew up. She sold trinkets and accepted donations, which I am reliably informed she donated to the RSPCA. Apparently, she's a cat person.

The first person she served on behalf of The Drifter was Grant Mahon.

"Would you like to make a donation?" she asked.

"Yes. I have a parcel for a particular child." he replied.

It was the expression he'd bought from King Rat. He handed her a parcel and the Charity Worker placed it immediately into a sport's bag at her feet.

"What can Santa bring for you?"

"I made a list."

He handed her an envelope. She glanced inside at a photograph of me. He'd written my name on the back.

"Happy Christmas." she said. "I hope you get the gift you asked for."

I can't confirm most of the following. Actually, I can't confirm any of it. However, when I imagine the scene, this is how I picture it. Feel free to add your own tense soundtrack and sinister lighting.

The Charity Worker boarded a train and sat on one side of a table. She'd reserved all four of its seats. She likes her alone time.

A man entered and sat opposite her. The rest of the train was quiet. As they whispered to each other, they looked out of the window and avoided eye contact. They have a history. They have a mutual mistrust.

"Before I give you the files, I want you to know this is for real." she said.

"There's something unusual?"

"I set up as normal, same process, same number. But when I checked the names and faces, they're all for the same guy."

"All four? What did this guy do?"

"I've never heard of him."

"I need to know. When I meet him, I want to know more about his last 12 months than he does."

He was true to his promise.

The next evening, he posed as a journalist and interviewed Caitlyn in a stylish wine bar. He dressed in a smart suit. He looked handsome, respectable and trustworthy. He had an open notebook and a line of questions.

The following morning, he planted a bug in a psychiatrist's office and listened to Aaron's latest session. He overheard Aaron's summary of his whole year.

Half an hour after the session ended, he entered King Rat's shop and placed an envelope of money on the counter. King Rat, ever the opportunistic individual, revealed everything he knew.

That afternoon, he looked scruffy in a rock band T-shirt and tattered jeans. He listened carefully to Gary's drunken, frenetic ravings and picked up the tab for all the drinks.

During the early evening rush hour, he hacked Grant Mahon's computer. He read every document and e-mail that mentioned Zara or me.

That night, he hid in Darren Rourke's car five minutes before Darren reached it. Darren didn't realize he had company until a hooded man placed a knife at his throat. Darren answered every question and offered to answer more.

These visits and activities took him less than 36 hours. Armed with these details, The Drifter knew more about my year than I did.

The final part of the scheme required my return to the city I had escaped three months earlier. My enemies needed me to ignore the risks I knew about and walk into the crosshairs of an even greater danger.

Aaron was the least anxious for a reunion, but he was the most creative. He spread a story that Caitlyn wanted to see me. My brother heard the lie and repeated it to me as an apology for everything he had ever said against her. He didn't know the story's origin.

I had no idea what I was walking into.

The dangerous, complicated life

Five buildings form the southern boundary of the city's downtown core. These buildings are also considered, rightly or wrongly, to be the only five in the city that will always be outside of Brad Doyle's influence. This is because one of the five is the regional headquarters for the police department.

You may wonder why it is that I talk about the city as if it still belongs to Doyle even though he has retired. This is for three reasons:

1. It's a long-standing habit. I've described it this way for most of my life.

2. He isn't retired in the conventional sense. He still has connections and he still has power. If his empire of assorted criminals were a software company, Doyle would be an honorary board member and a senior technical consultant.

3. It's a form of laziness. It's easier to equate an area with Doyle's control than trying to remember the confusing and evolving distribution of territory between his squabbling former lieutenants.

Maybe Doyle's influence on these five buildings was no different from his influence on the rest of the city. Maybe they carried a symbolic illusion of additional safety only. Either way, I planned to drive within their confines and restrict my brief homecoming to these five buildings only.

Actually, I wanted to restrict my visit to less than five because I hoped I wouldn't need the police station.

The other four buildings in this supposed safe zone are The Duke of York Hotel, The North Square Hotel, a shopping complex unimaginatively called The District and a plain, 15-storey structure known locally as City Tower.

The Duke of York is old and classy. They charge exorbitant prices and justify this through history and reputation. Most people consider it more expensive than it deserves. It was the last hotel in the city I would stay at by choice under any other circumstances, which made it the perfect place for me to stay.

The North Square, or The Square as the locals call it, is newer and popular with a younger demographic. They charge exorbitant prices and justify this through trends and fads. Most people consider it more expensive than it deserves.

The District is a series of reasonably expensive shops in a reasonably struggling city. It's an uncomfortable mix of thriving stores and empty stalls.

City Tower is a revolving door of agencies and firms. It offers cheaper rates and it's popular with small companies and start-ups. Nobody overstays his or her welcome and its occupants graduate to more prestigious locations or go bankrupt. The building itself changes names so frequently that nobody troubles themselves to learn each new title. At the time of my ill-considered return, it was also where Caitlyn worked.

I'd created a strategy and every part of my plan involved somewhere in this area. I drafted a list of rules that I believed would increase the likelihood of a successful visit.

1. Tell no one I was coming, not even the people I wanted to see.

2. Restrict my movements to the only five buildings that Brad Doyle has never claimed as territory.

3. Above all things, keep a low profile.

By successful, I mean that I would achieve my twin goals of a conversation with Caitlyn and a subsequent escape from the city with the approximate state of well-being in which I entered it. I thought these rules improved my chances of preserving my stubborn existence.

I particularly liked the third rule. I whispered its final two words to myself in the hope that saying them and hearing them repeatedly would reinforce my commitment to their overall philosophy.

On a theoretical level, I was proud of my plan. I liked my plan. I still think it has some merit. On a practical level, this is me we're talking about; events conspired against me before I even reached the outskirts.

I hit my first snag in the snarled traffic. It was my fault for trusting split-second precision to a plan that involved the city's ring road. It could have been worse. I could have trusted public transit. Never trust a complex plan to the punctuality of public transit.

On a side note, Skyfall is the kind of far-fetched, action-packed movie for which I have a weakness. I know it isn't intended seriously, but even it stretches credibility when James Bond's opponent relies on the timely arrival of a tube train. No international super-criminal would trust the success of his or her scheme to a British rail timetable.

I'm sorry. I'm digressing and I wanted to tell you the story of how my efforts to repair my broken plan inadvertently shattered it beyond all recognition.

I missed the start of Caitlyn's lunch and my philosophy of low profile didn't align with walking into the 27 places she might potentially be eating. Instead, I decided to check in at my hotel and then linger near City Tower for her return. I entered The Duke of York's main lobby and my ailing strategy suffered another setback.

I walked to the front desk and the clerk greeted me with a warm smile that suggested she had never seen my face before under any circumstances. This made me happy because complete ignorance of my entire life is my favourite quality in strangers. I cautiously allowed confidence in my plan to return and then someone shouted my name. I turned and saw Zack Regan running towards me.

He delivered questions without pause. Why was I here? Was Tessa here? Was I Tessa's boyfriend? Did Tom know? Was he jealous?

Zack fired them rapidly, barely pausing for breath, never pausing to allow for an answer. He arrived opposite me with an idiotic grin and pushed his face into mine confrontationally. He continued to deliver his quick-fire list of questions. I received a clear picture of his future headline, courtesy of his pre-written answers and his pre-determined story.

My plan needed a low profile. Everything depended on a low profile. I whispered these two words to myself in the hope that saying them and hearing them would reinforce my commitment to the overall philosophy.

I abandoned the philosophy and slammed my forehead into his face.

I used the time between leaving The Duke and arriving at City Tower to check in at The North Square using the last of my cash and a fake name. The grumpy clerk either hated his job or recognised me; I didn't ask which.

I found a secluded spot near City Tower's main entrance with a line of sight to the door. The pillar I leaned against hid me from The Duke and the ambulance parked outside it.

I tried to solve the mystery of whatever mistake I'd committed. My best guess was that Zack Regan had a contact at the studio that provided details of Tessa's travel bookings. That was how he always seemed to know where Tom and Tessa might be. That was why he'd arrived at The Duke expecting to see Tessa. I made a mental note to warn her the next time we spoke. I made another mental note to warn the studio I'd abandoned their rental car in The Duke's underground parking garage.

I tried and failed to restore my faith in my plan. It is fair to say that my confidence didn't return because it would have been hypocritical to believe there were no consequences to assaulting a journalist while simultaneously restricting my view of events that might remind me of this setback.

My plan had fallen apart more than I realised. I didn't care because Caitlyn was walking towards the tower.

She looked relaxed. I knew instantly that she'd found what she'd set out to find one year earlier. The worry was gone from her face. The tension had left her stance and her shoulders. She was smiling, happily and sincerely. She'd never looked more beautiful.

I suddenly wished I hadn't returned. If my arrival placed her newfound happiness at risk, I wanted to be somewhere else. I didn't get the opportunity. She looked in my direction before I could slip away and her smile widened. She walked over to join me.

"Hello … I … I'm sorry. I wasn't expecting to see you."

"It's a surprise." I said.

"It's a good surprise. I heard you'd moved away."

"I'm back for one day and I wanted to see you. I'm sorry. I should have called first."

"It's fine. I wanted to see you too. You look well."

"Thanks. You look great."

She leaned across and we embraced clumsily. It was embarrassing and awkward, as if I'd never held her before.

"How have you been?" I said.

"I concentrated on those other things, like I said I would. It turns out most jobs don't pay enough, most bosses are difficult, and my friends and family will always let me down."

"Sorry."

"Don't be. You were right. I had to find out for myself."

"You seem happy."

"I am. I think the past 12 months were good for me. They weren't good in the way I expected, but they helped me figure things out. … I've been thinking about us. A journalist came to see me about you."

"Sorry about that."

"No, it's OK. It brought back memories. For a long time, I remembered the bad times. He helped me remember the good stuff."

"What did you tell him?"

"I told him I let you go and it was a mistake."

"I thought you wanted to move on."

"I'm not sure I knew what I wanted. You didn't seem sure either. You'd ask to meet me, stand me up, and then you'd make up these elaborate, unbelievable excuses."

"It's been a strange year."

"Forget about the last year. You shouldn't have lied to me about the dangerous, complicated life you claimed to be living. It was a mistake, but I made mistakes too. And before all of this, things were really great."

"Yes, they were."

"Are you seeing anybody?"

"No. Are you?"

"No. Oh, but I am late for work. I really want to talk to you some more. Where are you staying?"

I took out my key cards for The North Square. They were still in a small envelope with the hotel name and room number printed on the outside. I kept one card for myself. I passed the second card and the envelope to Caitlyn.

"How about I call for you later?" she said. "I could be there for seven."

A scenario that involves lives not ending

In keeping with my rules and a renewed interest in a low profile, I decided to return to The North Square and stay there until Caitlyn's visit. I could see The Square's front entrance 100 yards away, an elaborate façade that hung over the outside lane of the road. All that stood between relative safety and me was a walk of two blocks.

I crossed the street from the corner near City Tower to the corner near The District, dodging impatient traffic as I went. I stepped onto the pavement and found my route blocked by Anna Dash returning from her lunch. Anna works in City Tower. I probably should have worked that out earlier.

She started to cry and then slapped me across the cheek.

"How could you? How?"

I paused to consider my response. I didn't want to disrespect her feelings. Then again, she was blaming me for the fictional murder of a woman who didn't really exist by a character played by an actor who wasn't me.

"Anna. It is Anna, isn't it? I can't really talk now, but, seriously, *it's a TV show*."

I heard Gary's approach from behind me before I saw him. He channelled the frustration of months spent not attacking me into a strange guttural scream. I sidestepped instinctively as he dived. Anna didn't. His shoulder struck her stomach and he tackled her to the ground like a rugby player.

I stepped away as a crowd of onlookers sprang to her defence. I walked east past The District's southern entrance and made it within thirty feet of The Square's front entrance. I saw a car drift from amongst the westbound traffic and I ducked into an alley a second before Aaron's tiny hatchback mounted the pavement I'd recently vacated.

I fled down the path and passed underneath the walkway that connected The District to The North Square. I could hear Aaron perform an inefficient nine-point turn as he tried to turn his car towards the alley. Before he could resume his pursuit, I ducked past some smokers and through the fire door they'd propped open.

I climbed to The District's second floor via the first available escalator. I checked the glass walkway between the complex and the hotel and discovered that the doors opened from the hotel side only. I crossed to the other side of The District using a pedestrian bridge.

I wanted somewhere I could stay out of sight. Without thinking through the wisdom of the decision, I ducked through the nearest doorway and entered a sports bar.

It was almost empty and its walls held four times as many televisions as customers. The three patrons at the bar, each with their back to me, grumbled about the absent barman until the picture changed in front of them. Every television in the room returned from the commercial break to resume the summary of their soccer team's year. The highlight reel portrayed one disappointment after another in a series of six-second clips and their complaints switched topic.

"This whole season's a disaster."

"It would be different if we had Max Cane in midfield."

"I want to meet the guy who broke his leg and I want to kill him."

I belatedly thought through the wisdom of my decision and concluded that I didn't want to be in a sports bar after all. I slowly backed out as the photograph my mother had presented to Zack Regan appeared on every monitor, including the 60-inch screen over the bar.

As I turned, the first face I saw was Grant Mahon's. He was climbing the escalator I'd used one minute earlier. His eyes scanned the storey for any sign of me. I used the ten seconds before he reached the second floor to jump on the escalator parallel to his own. I pushed my way past the ambling shoppers who littered the descending staircase. I heard cries of protest behind me as Grant did the same.

I exited through the nearest doors and returned to the pavement. I glanced right and saw Aaron's car turn the corner. I turned left. In these few moments, Grant recovered six seconds of the ten I'd stolen for my head start.

As I turned the corner, I almost crashed into the crowd that were comforting the shaken Anna Dash and loudly criticizing the culpable Gary Grey. I skilfully dodged most of the group. Grant burst around the corner and ploughed straight into them.

We collapsed in a heap and got in each other's way as we tried to stand simultaneously. Gary saw me and lunged through the crowd. He missed me and connected with almost everyone else. Anna lost her balance and stumbled backwards. She swept her arms through a dramatic arc in a doomed attempt to regain her balance and delivered a perfect elbow into Grant Mahon's nose that knocked him into the road.

He pulled himself to his feet, pulled a gun from his jacket and aimed into the crowd. He forgot me temporarily and searched for the woman who'd struck him. As he found his target, somebody screamed and Anna froze. Then, in an act of spontaneous heroism and perfect timing, Aaron Hayes ran him over in his comically small car.

We held our breath until we saw evidence of Mahon's survival. When we received it, part of me regretted it wasn't a bigger vehicle. It's a less than charitable admission, but my disappointment in the automobile to person weight ratio sums up my opinion of Mahon so perfectly that I can't resist the urge to quote it.

The crowd gasped, Anna feinted and I disappeared through the next available door. I entered the shopping complex I'd entered and abandoned once already. I took the escalator to the second storey, but this time avoided the sports bar. I checked the walkway to the hotel. It was still locked.

I stayed close to the pedestrian bridge and monitored the exits for any sign of people who wished me harm. I tried to identify what had happened in the past hour that could have brought this diverse group of men in my direction. Then, in a flash of inspiration, I knew.

It was King Rat. It had to be. They all knew King Rat and King Rat knew everything. He probably knew the officers who'd responded to reports of Zack Regan's assault. He'd probably sold this information to everyone he thought might pay for it. If I was right, I could guess the identities of everyone he'd called and I knew who'd received the first call. I immediately looked for Darren Rourke or anyone who might work for him.

I saw Darren before he saw me and I ducked back from his line of sight. If he had company, and I predicted three violent associates, sneaking out of The District was going to be difficult. If they knew I was here and they covered the four main exits, I was trapped.

I plotted a path to the roof.

I knew it was possible. Three years earlier, I'd met an old school friend for lunch and he'd taken me to his office in City Tower to show me the view. We'd spotted a dozen people on The District's roof, including smokers, mobile users on private calls and an affectionate couple who hadn't objected to the tower's audience.

The staircase sat behind a plain, unwelcoming door. I found it between a map that didn't reference it and a passport photo booth. I wanted to disappear behind it before anyone else found me. I was too late.

He was big. He was punch through walls big. He was punch through conventionally sized people for fun big.

Perhaps it relied on unscientific stereotypes to assume that he worked for Darren. It was probably prejudicial of me to make unproven judgments based on his appearance. In my defence, it wasn't prejudicial of me to base the same conclusions on his accusatory stare, his finger pointing and his repeated yelling of Darren's name.

I slammed into the door and snapped it past the weak lock they'd installed at some point in the past three years. I climbed two flights and reached the roof. I immediately initiated a search for my next escape route.

I belatedly considered the wisdom of running to a destination with a giant assailant in pursuit when the original advantage of that destination was as a hiding place whose existence was unknown to assailants of any size. I belatedly considered the wisdom of considering so many of my day's important decisions belatedly.

I discovered that the staircase I had used to reach this area was the only staircase for this purpose. I leaned over the edge and searched for a ladder that could return me to the street. Four men stood at the top of the staircase by the time I located the ladder on the west end of the northern wall. There was no chance of me reaching it before they reached me.

Darren led the group. He was followed by a group of men whose respective size, shape and aesthetic failings I'd come to expect.

"How did you know I was back?" I asked.

I wanted it to sound like an honest enquiry and not like a desperate grab for more thinking time.

"The Rat phoned me." Darren replied. "King Rat knows everything."

He tried to make it sound like an honest answer and not like an opportunity for his colleagues to spread across the width of the roof. He stayed in his position near the top of the staircase as they walked towards me. In response, I selected the best of the options I'd analysed, criticized and discounted.

"In all sincerity, I can't wish you a happy new year." I said.

"Why is that?" he replied.

"I'm going to get away. When I do… it won't be fun to be you."

I sprinted away from them. As I reached the eastern edge of the roof, I leapt into empty sky and fell fifteen feet. I landed on the glass ceiling of the walkway that connected The District to North Square.

I heard an ominous crack in the glass beneath me, but it didn't break. This was a relief because its immediate collapse was something I'd considered a real and dangerous possibility. I didn't hear the ominous crack from my ankle because the ominous crack from the glass drowned it out.

Fifteen feet and a sheet of glass kept me from the walkway. Thirty feet and serious doubts about my ability to survive the fall unscathed kept me from the alley. I edged across the walkway and towards the hotel. I carefully avoided the uneven joints that attached the panes together.

Ugly was the first to brave the jump. He landed awkwardly on one of the joints. Tall tried it next and landed awkwardly on Ugly. Big tried it last. He missed both Tall and Ugly and went straight through the weakened glass into the corridor below. The other panes followed, one at a time, like a destructive domino topple. I dropped as the last glass sheet fell and landed badly on my unhappy ankle.

I limped slowly into the hotel and made it as far as the elevator. A sign at the far end of the corridor indicated a staircase that I couldn't reach quickly. Instead, I pressed the button and waited.

I heard the groans of Darren's colleagues and guessed my pursuers had fallen in number from four to one. I heard Darren drop onto the bridge as the elevator arrived, the only one of us to do so without injury. I got in and pressed for lobby. The doors closed before Darren reached me.

When the doors opened, I found myself face to face with Gary Grey. In the confusion of the car accident, he'd snuck away from the crowd and picked up Grant Mahon's gun. He held it close to his body as I stepped out of the lift and allowed the doors to close.

"There's no one here to save you this time." he said.

The people behind him couldn't see the weapon. No one but us knew the danger I was in. The elevator ascended the shaft.

"This is the way it's supposed to finish." he continued. "I don't know what you did to upset those other people, but they're late to the game. I was here first. It's supposed to finish with me."

"I don't suppose you'd consider a scenario that involves lives not ending?"

"I don't think so, no."

I thought of the year's incidents. I smiled as I remembered Gary driving down the staircase towards the river.

"It's really been a year, hasn't it Gary?"

"It's really been a year." he agreed.

"I'm sorry for what's happened." I said. "I know you think that I lied to my sister about you. I didn't, but I'm sorry all of this came from that."

"We can't talk this out now. There's been too much."

"I know." I said as the elevator doors opened behind me. "So, shoot me already."

I dropped to the floor as Gary pulled the trigger. Darren returned fire from behind me. I buried my body into the carpet as much as possible as the lobby fell into panic and emptied.

I glanced at Darren and then at Gary. Neither of them glanced back. Both men had successfully hit the other several times and they'd switched their respective attentions to personal matters such as bullet wounds and associated pain.

I didn't know what the police response rate might be for an incident two buildings away from a regional headquarters, but I suspected it might be swift. I spent the thirty seconds perfecting an unconventional and reasonably effective crawl. I progressed to an injured limp and left through the back door as the police ran in the front.

I hobbled painfully from the back of The North Square. I hesitated as I reached the border of a hypothetical safe zone that hadn't provided much in the way of safety. The sound of police sirens gave me a well-timed incentive and I crossed the street.

It started to rain.

I turned up my collar and tucked my arms tightly into my chest. I vaguely noticed the car with tinted windows as it passed in the opposite direction. I missed the U-turn the car completed to return in my direction. I finally gave it the attention it deserved as it slowed to a halt alongside me.

The front passenger door opened and a man climbed out. He had a physique that seemed suitable for a career in hurting people.

"Get in the car."

Maybe it was instinct and maybe it was his Eastern European accent, but I took a step backwards. Some of the city's eastern Europeans work for The Russian, the most vicious of Brad Doyle's former lieutenants.

"I'm OK walking." I said.

It was obvious to everyone there that I wasn't OK walking.

The man took a gun from his jacket and sighed. He wasn't interested in expanding the conversation beyond its initial, limited scope.

"You really need to get in the car."

I stepped in, sat on the back seat and closed my door. The man with the gun climbed into the back alongside me. I stated the case for the defence immediately.

"Please, whoever you are, this will be a misunderstanding. It happens to me all the time. I'm not who you think I am."

"Sure you are." he replied. "You're Warwick Ray's little brother. Brad Doyle says Hi."

He hit me in the head with the handle of his gun. I don't remember the rest of the journey.

A lucky man or a dead man

I woke up in a derelict warehouse. I could hear the rain pounding the metal roof as the city progressed from a shower to a downpour. There was light somewhere behind me, but it didn't reach my part of the building. I was in a chair, my arms tied behind me.

I heard two men talking in the distance, probably from somewhere near the limited light. I couldn't see them. I suspected one of the voices belonged to the man who'd ushered me into the car.

"... look for three weeks. The day after we give up, we find him."

"I heard when we couldn't find him, Doyle hired The Drifter to look."

"He should be grateful we found him. Anything's better than meeting that serial psycho."

"Are they going to kill him?"

"Doyle thinks if he kills the brother, Warwick will run, Ned won't testify, and the whole case will fall apart."

"Who is Markov sending?"

"Nobody. He's coming himself."

"Markov's coming? The poor guy might have been better off with The Drifter."

Andrei Markov is The Russian. You probably guessed that already.

I expected him to ask about my brother's location. I was scared what would happen when I couldn't answer. I skilfully presented myself with more time to consider this conundrum by falling back into unconsciousness.

I had nightmares that didn't do justice to my probable fate.

I woke again, still dazed, a little more conscious than earlier. The pain in my head faded and the pain in my ankle returned. The conversation behind me continued.

"And he said 'I knew the Russians would get him.' And I thought to myself 'Are we all Russians now?' Is that what we are? Is that what people think?"

"We work for a Russian."

"We do and he's called The Russian because he's Russian. I'm not Russian. I'm Latvian. You're Georgian. Think about who else we work with. We have Estonians. We have Moldovans. We have … Where is Jaak from?"

"I think he's Finnish."

"That's right. So, we have Finns. We have a Serbian."

"We do? Who's Serbian?"

"Nik."

"Which one is Nik?"

"The crazy one we don't like."

"He's Serbian? I thought he was Russian."

"Everyone thinks he's Russian. Everyone thinks we're all Russian. We work for The Russian. We must be Russians. It's so disrespectful."

"I think our guest woke up."

"He did. Good. He can tell us what we need to know."

The Latvian dragged his chair across the concrete floor. He made no effort to lift it and its legs scraped loudly as he approached. He placed it one metre in front of me and sat down. The other kidnapper stood behind him.

The Latvian stared at me. Either he was trying to read my expression or inspecting the wound he'd inflicted to the side of my head.

"Look at me." he said. "Look … at … me!"

I raised my face slightly and returned his gaze. He waited until he had my full attention and then he asked his question.

"Do I look Russian to you?"

I searched for as tactful an answer as my fuzzy brain could muster.

"With all due respect to you and your country of birth, I would suggest you look Eastern European, but I would lack the confidence and requisite ability to be any more specific."

My kidnappers looked at each other.

"I like that answer."

"It was a good answer."

"It was very respectful."

"I noticed that too."

I was pleased they had noticed. I'd specifically aimed for politeness. The usual rules of etiquette state that you are not required to extend etiquette to everyone and the list of who it doesn't extend to includes people who would happily kill you, unless they are currently attempting to kill you and the extension of etiquette might persuade them in not doing so, in which case this is an exception to the previously referenced exception and etiquette applies once more.

We heard a door slam and a third man joined us. His name was Kirin and I knew him by reputation. He was The Russian's closest associate.

"Kirin, why does everyone think we're all Russians?" the Latvian asked.

"No one thinks we're all Russians. They say we're all Russians because it's faster to say 'The Russians' than 'Those People who Work for The Russian'."

"Doesn't that bother you?"

"Why would it bother me? I'm Russian."

Kirin switched his focus to me.

"When did he wake up?"

"Two minutes ago." the Latvian replied.

"Markov's finishing a call. You should get out of here. He's in a bad mood."

The Latvian and the Georgian left the room. I suspected I'd soon be nostalgic for a time when my kidnappers were more interested in the countries with which they were incorrectly associated.

As their footsteps faded, I heard another set come closer. An older, heavier man sat in the chair opposite me. I'd never met him before, but I knew who he was.

His right cheek included a deep knife wound that had healed untidily. The left side of his face carried a burn mark from his ear to the shoulder. I knew from local tradition that The Russian refused to answer questions about the origins of either wound, presumably because the men who'd inflicted them were now the victims of unsolved murder investigations.

He lit a cigarette and smoked it slowly. We sat in silence while the light flickered across his face. He was the most terrifying man I'd ever met.

"There are people who think you're a problem." he said finally. "They want me to solve you. How I solve you is up to me."

Kirin hovered on his employer's shoulder and said nothing. I wondered how many times he'd seen Markov interrogate a problem. I wondered how many of those problems had survived the discussion.

"There are two ways to do this." Markov continued. "We can bargain for your release or send a message with your death. I can make either work. It makes no difference to me. It makes a big difference to you."

He leaned in and gave me a better view of his scars.

"What do you think you will be? Are you a lucky man or a dead man?"

I didn't reply. Markov looked more closely as he considered my fate and his expression changed.

"Why do I know you?" he asked.

He let the sudden confusion unsettle him.

"What is it?" Kirin asked. "Is he a lucky man or a dead man?"

Markov produced a serrated hunting knife from his jacket pocket and passed it to his colleague.

"I think … he will be … my hero."

My head snapped to attention. This was not the answer I'd expected.

"I didn't place the name." Markov said "They said it was Warwick's younger brother."

"Is there a problem?" Kirin asked.

"You don't recognise him?"

"I don't recognize him."

"This is Nehemiah Ray. This is the man who broke Max Cane's leg."

"... I don't believe it. You're right."

The two men started to switch between English and Russian haphazardly, but I caught the words travesty, world cup, offside and stupid German linesman. While Markov continued to jabber about injustice and corruption, Kirin cut my ropes and helped me to my feet. They dragged my injured body to The Russian's car. They let me ride alone in the back seat.

They drove me to my hotel and begged me to tell them the story of the accident. They asked me on nine separate occasions to repeat the part where I landed on Max Cane. Each time I told it, they laughed louder than the time before.

We concluded the journey with the two Russians telling each other an abbreviated version of the tale using sound effects only. If you are wondering, this approximates to "bang-bang, bang-bang, whee-aarrgghh, splat!" and in a Russian accent.

They dropped me at the hotel's rear entrance. They flashed a smile at me as if we were old friends. They waved as if wishing me well was perfectly normal. I heard the sound effects and the laughter resume as they drove away.

I stood silently as they left. My brain needed a minute to process what had happened. A large group of New Year revellers walked past me, singing as they went. Visually, I was a mess, but they barely noticed me.

I looked at my watch. It was 7:40.

I remembered what Caitlyn had said about my outrageous, unbelievable excuses. This would be tough to explain.

I avoided the lobby and pulled myself up three flights of stairs. It took twenty minutes to reach my floor.

I entered my suite without any of the cautiousness or care that I'm accustomed to taking. I was tired. I was in pain. I presumed that Caitlyn, already sensitive about the times I had stood her up, would have been and gone.

If you want to be glass half full about the situation, it was a great room. The North Square changed my opinion in that regard. If you can afford to stay there, I definitely recommend it.

I threw my jacket on one of the two sofas in the living area. I weighed up the merits of cleaning myself up in the bathroom to the right or collapsing in the bedroom through the double doors to the left. I decided that if I reached a bed, I might not get up for some time. I went to the bathroom.

I opened the door and immediately saw Caitlyn on the floor, her back to the shower door, a gag in her mouth, her knees near her chin and her wrists bound to her ankles. I hesitated as our eyes met. I smiled to reassure her, but didn't convince either one of us.

The bedroom doors opened and a man took a seat on one of the sofas. He was my age, my height and my build. There was something of a post-Beatles John Lennon to his appearance.

You could start by not killing me

"Do you know who I am?" he said.

His accent was a confused muddle that suggested a lifetime spent in different parts of the world.

"I can guess. The Drifter?"

"I never liked that name much. You can call me Sean."

"Thank you."

He invited me to sit on the other sofa by casually waving at it with his gun. I slowly limped to the seat and sat down.

"How did you find me?" I asked.

"The clerk on the front desk recognized you, something to do with a newspaper column about the hotel industry. He entered Mal McCall in brackets after the fake name you provided."

"Thank you for the explanation." I said appreciatively. "I know you don't have to tell me anything."

I'd considered politeness a priority during my conversation with various criminals of Eastern European descent. I still considered it important for comparable reasons.

"I'm impressed with how calm you were when you saw me." he said.

"It's a skill you develop over time when attempts on your life prove as frequent as they do in mine."

"Yes, it does seem like your involvement in these types of incidents has become remarkably commonplace."

"Commonplace? I like that. It's a nice word for it."

"I'm sure you have a lot of questions, but I have to wait for instructions before we do this. I wasn't expecting your female visitor. She's not part of the deal."

"You could let her go. She's not involved in this."

"It's not my decision. I should be getting a phone call, but we could be waiting for a few hours."

I looked down at my shoes for a moment as I tried to regain my composure and plan my strategy.

"OK. What do we talk about?"

"You could tell me the story of your year. I've done some research, but I'm still not sure why a nice guy like you is sitting here with me."

"I could do that."

"Where were you 12 months ago?" Sean asked.

"I was in a bar with Caitlyn and her friends celebrating New Year."

"And you had no idea what the year would bring you?"

"No one could have predicted my year."

"Did you make any resolutions then?"

"No. All I wanted was someone to share my life with, a job I enjoyed and minimal contact with the more irritating members of my family. For a brief moment, I had all three."

"When did it start to go wrong?"

"Looking back, there were probably clues on New Year's Day, but I missed them. No, it really hit on January 4th."

I told him the story I just told you. Sean filled in some of the details I didn't know, including the ones I've repeated to you. Sean was surprisingly informative for a man who'd been paid to kill me.

If I ignored the unusual circumstances, and I confess that ignoring them was a challenge, there was a lot to like about Sean. He was talkative. He listened attentively. There was something inherently cool about him. I tried to focus on these aspects because they scared me less than pondering how many people he'd killed.

It was probably a lot.

We heard noises from outside the building as the crowds spilled onto the street for midnight. They loudly provided a narration of the current time, not exclusively for our reference, but certainly to our advantage.

We started to consider resolutions. I suppose it was a traditional turn in the conversation. The calendar reaches its conclusion and everyone switches his or her attention to the approaching year.

"Can I get in early and wish you a Happy New Year?" I asked.

"A Happy New Year to you too."

"Have you made any resolutions?"

"I always seem to work the holidays. I should take more time off."

"I guess every career has its downsides." I replied sympathetically.

He glanced at his phone, wishing it would ring, as he'd done every two minutes for the past twenty.

"How about you? Any resolutions?"

"I've got three." I confirmed.

"Are any of them 'not dying'?" Sean asked.

"Actually, they're all along that theme. I'm thinking of going with not dying, not almost dying and not provoking anyone to wish I'd die."

He nodded approvingly and then dismissed them completely.

"Yeah? Good luck with that."

We heard another shout from outside as the time neared midnight and the gathering crowds started their countdown. It was difficult to place a number on how many had congregated outside the hotel. From the volume, I estimated hundreds.

I didn't move. I was on the far end of the couch in roughly the same position and posture I'd occupied for four hours. I still wore my charming smile and I still sported a bruise to an aching head wound. I was trying to look relaxed, but I was exhausted. It had been a difficult year. It had been a very difficult day.

Sean glanced at his phone as the clock's display echoed the shouts of the people outside. New Year celebrations built to a climax as the crowd announced midnight's arrival. We both remained seated. We both remained calm.

"I'm really sorry about this." Sean said.

"No, please. Take your time."

Sean looked at his phone again as if a message might have arrived in the previous five seconds.

"This job can be so frustrating." he complained.

"If it's bothering you so much, you should consider a career change, perhaps stop killing people. Hey, you could start by not killing me."

I looked for a reaction, hoped for a momentary grin and caught one.

"Nice try." Sean said.

I leaned forward from the wall, far enough to display my seriousness and not enough to appear threatening.

"If you let Caitlyn go, she could disappear. You could keep the money and no one would know. You don't have to keep your word to this man."

It was my fifth attempt to bargain for Caitlyn's life.

"You think you know who hired me?"

"Not exactly." I admitted. "I've got it narrowed to a shortlist of people."

"Here's a clue. 14 days ago, I was paid to kill you. Then, ten days ago, I was paid to kill you. Independently of those payments, six days ago I was paid to kill you. I've never seen a duplicate order and then you happen. Do you know how unpopular you are?"

"It's slowly dawning on me."

"Who are you thinking?"

"I'm thinking Grant Mahon, Aaron Hayes and Darren Rourke. Gary wants me dead more than they do, but I doubt he can afford your prices."

"Guess what happened two days ago."

"Brad Doyle paid you to kill me."

"I'm very impressed."

Sean's phone rang and instantly ended our conversation. I listened for clues and received ambiguities in response.

"Hello. … Yes. … Yes. … Understood."

He disconnected the call.

"Do you care about her?" Sean asked.

"Yes."

"You'll do exactly what I say."

"Yes." I replied, though it might not have been a question.

Sean motioned me towards the bathroom. He followed several steps behind. I looked around the corner at my ex-girlfriend.

"Untie her. Remove the gag. Keep her quiet." Sean instructed.

I kneeled down beside Caitlyn and whispered in her ear.

"You have to stay calm. OK?"

Caitlyn nodded. She looked scared. I pulled the gag away from her mouth and untied her wrists and ankles.

"All the stories you told me were true?" she said, the only question whose answer explained everything that had happened.

I smiled weakly and nodded. I tried hard to hide the fear from my expression. I didn't succeed.

"Is he going to kill us?" she whispered.

"I don't know." I replied.

As good a place as any to think

We took the elevator to the lobby. At Sean's insistence, we walked slowly to the far corner of the hotel's car park. Caitlyn's legs hurt from her hours tied up in the bathroom. I limped on an ankle that was twice its usual size. We leaned on each other and this only complicated our progress.

Sean followed patiently behind us. He made no effort to hide the gun in his hand and drew stares from the people still celebrating. Even in their drunken state, they knew something was very wrong. They watched us walk by and they said nothing.

We reached Sean's car. He told Caitlyn to climb into the driver's seat and I sat alongside her. Sean climbed into the back.

"Why is it important to you that we're seen?" I asked.

"I need the police to list you as missing and presumed dead." he explained.

I wished I hadn't asked.

Caitlyn drove to the ring road and circled around to where it cuts through the woods. We travelled in silence. I considered and discarded one escape plan after another.

"Stop here" Sean said.

I saw a steep slope fifty yards ahead of us and I realised we were close to where Zara Mahon had hit me with her car.

"Thank you again for the story." Sean said. "Someone like me can't help but be intrigued by a man who has so many attempts on his life. Your file is fascinating."

He didn't say story. He said file. It was only one word, but I immediately knew we were safe.

"It's time to leave." Sean said. "I promised she could take you from here."

"Who?" Caitlyn asked.

A back door opened and Audrey White climbed in. She placed a suitcase on the back seat between her and Sean.

"You're late." she said.

"Don't put this on me. It took them four hours to reach a decision." Sean replied.

"Is that what they said? There's no way they discussed this that long. I bet they couldn't track down one of the stakeholders because it's New Year."

"I hate working holidays."

"Tell me about it."

Audrey turned to face her hostages.

"Hi Ray."

I didn't reply. Although I'd predicted Audrey's arrival, my brain was still trying to guess what awaited us.

"And you must be Caitlyn. We almost met once in a restaurant. You may not remember; it was a long time ago. My name is Audrey and I work for the United States government."

"Hi." Caitlyn replied on autopilot.

"Caitlyn, do you want the good news or the bad news?"

"I really need some good news."

"You're wondering what's going to happen to you. They've argued about it, but they've made a decision. I have permission to tell you that decision."

"Have you got this?" Sean said.

"Sure. Happy New Year." Audrey replied.

"Happy New Year."

She passed him her car keys and Sean climbed out.

"Did you guess who that was?" Audrey asked me.

"He's CIA. You've captured The Drifter and Sean's acting the part so nobody works that out."

"I'm impressed. I'm beginning to think you picked the wrong career."

"If you've caught The Drifter, why take assignments?"

"We want his contacts. We want his accountants. We want his suppliers. He won't talk and that's a pity, but we'll get them anyway if everyone believes The Drifter is still available for hire."

"To maintain the illusion, you'd have to complete his assignments."

"National security has to outweigh individual rights."

"I hope that's a joke." Caitlyn said.

"It's not a joke, but I do like its punch line. Ray, you want to take a guess?"

"They're not going to kill us, but they need people to believe we're dead. That's why Sean wanted people to see us outside the hotel. Where are you taking us?"

"We have some houses on a tropical island. It would be house arrest, but the house is on the beach, the beach is on the pacific, the weather is beautiful and the view is amazing."

"This doesn't feel right." I said. "Things don't go my way."

"I know the year you've had. If anyone deserves this, it's you."

"What about me?" Caitlyn asked Audrey.

"I know a lot has happened to you tonight. You were tied up. You were kidnapped. You've got a lot to think through, but isn't paradise as good a place as any to think?"

Caitlyn didn't reply and Audrey provided some further persuasion.

"Caitlyn, we need you on this. If you cooperate, we'll give you all the money Sean took as payment in the past year."

"How much money?" I asked.

Audrey nodded at the suitcase sitting alongside her and then continued her sales pitch to Caitlyn.

"A year ago you told Ray you needed to break up with him. Stressful work? You don't need to work anymore. Unreliable friends? Make new ones. Money? Trust me, you're OK. And if you haven't realised what a great guy you've got, you don't deserve him."

Caitlyn turned to look at me.

"What do you think?" I asked.

Caitlyn, still scared and confused, attempted a smile.

"How much money?" she said.

Fading into obscurity

This tale was always as much about the people in my life as it was about me. The story doesn't exist without these characters. Before I tell you what happened to me, I want to share what happened to them.

The police arrested Gary Grey for multiple charges. They released him after three of his uncles manipulated the investigation. They later rearrested and convicted him along with three of his uncles. I am told that Gary and his uncles no longer speak. The detective credited with securing the evidence against the corrupt police officers was previously a gang liaison officer.

Aaron Hayes became a local celebrity, a recipient of contentious acclaim and a poster boy for vigilante justice. He's currently dating Anna Dash's grateful daughter.

Due to Mal McCall's unpopularity, his newspaper released him from his contract to pursue other opportunities, although they never explained how a fictional person pursues other opportunities. Mal is fading into obscurity, ably assisted by the fact he never really existed.

Darren Rourke was arrested for attempted murder. He is currently in prison where he has learned he's not as tough as he thought he was.

Grant Mahon was arrested for attempted murder. His conviction was a significantly negative factor in his divorce settlement.

Zara Mahon successfully re-invented herself as the founder of a charity that specializes in women's rights. She funds the venture using the money she received from her divorce settlement.

Brad Doyle went to prison as a result of Ned Dwyer's testimony. Ned Dwyer escaped charges under the terms of his deal and he is in hiding from those loyal to Brad Doyle.

My brother never testified. However, in gratitude for his role in Brad Doyle's downfall, the witness protection program set him up with a new identity on the other side of the country. His search for his Spare Woman continues, assisted by his newfound ability to meet more than one woman per year. He remains the only member of my family to know of my survival, courtesy of a tip from Audrey White.

Audrey returned to America and received rave reviews for her research paper. She is now an acknowledged expert in improvised responses to unplanned acts of violence. She's joined the security detail for a Senator from an obscure American state.

Max Cane recovered from his injury and achieved even greater sporting success. His fans in Thailand are very happy.

Anna Dash is no longer obsessed with Tom Lincoln and Never After. She is now obsessed with a different star from a different show.

Tessa Caron returned to Never After as her former character's evil, long lost, identical twin sister. As part of her comeback deal, she murdered Tom Lincoln's character in her first story arc.

Esther Carson sold her house in the country and moved in with Tessa. She still doesn't like Tessa's friends, career or television show, but she's decided that she likes Tessa.

I am no longer three of the ten most hated people in Britain. I am 27th, 55th and 71st respectively. I'm more comfortable with the list now that there are more people ahead of me.

As I write this, Caitlyn Asher is alongside me. We have a beach. We have a beautiful view. More than either of these, she is the reason I am smiling. She is smiling too.

Last week, we received permission from the US government to return to Britain. They are confident that they have captured The Drifter's contacts and they don't need to keep our survival a secret anymore. We've yet to take them up on their offer.

I don't know what our future holds. I don't know where we will go. If you've enjoyed my story, I hope you wish us luck. What I do know is that whatever we choose, it will be somewhere that doesn't threaten media interest, violent retribution or dinner invitations.

THE END

Printed in Great Britain
by Amazon